D1215056

THE IMPOSSIBLE PROOF

The Impossible

FARRAR, STRAUS & GIROUX

NEW YORK

Proof

by HANS ERICH NOSSACK

Translated from the German by Michael Lebeck

PT
2627
0759
U53

LIBRARY
FLORIDA STATE UNIVERSITY
TALLAHASSEE, FLORIDA

Copyright © 1968 by Farrar, Straus and Giroux, Inc.

All rights reserved

Library of Congress catalog card number: 68–14912

Translated from the German *Unmögliche Beweisaufnahme*.
Originally published in the volume, *Spirale. Roman einer
schlaflosen Nacht,* © Suhrkamp Verlag, Frankfurt am Main, 1956

Published simultaneously in Canada by Ambassador Books, Ltd.,
Rexdale, Ontario

First printing, 1968

Printed in the United States of America

ROBERT MANNING
STROZIER LIBRARY

AUG 20 1991

Tallahassee, Florida

THE IMPOSSIBLE PROOF

ROBERT MANNING
STROZIER LIBRARY

AUG   1981

Tallahassee, Florida

Something which happened to a man is keeping him awake. He attempts to think his life through—backward to its beginnings, forward to its end. He tries his own case, taking all the parts; accuses, defends, and asks pardon, to find rest at last. Yet, each time his spiraling thoughts seem on the verge of going under in sleep, they strike a new fragment of his life, and once again they rise up into the merciless twilight of insomnia.

Perhaps this man will finally have to give up his struggle and stand shivering at the window. Outside, a new day is dawning and the birds have begun to chirp.

ASKED, after the charge had been read out, if he would plead guilty, the defendant answered that he was afraid he still could not decide.

And what did he mean by that?

By that he meant that he was still unable to judge whether he really would save the Court work by pleading guilty; it might be thought presumptuous of him if he were to anticipate the Court in this fashion. But if the Court were to find him guilty, he would have no objection.

The defendant had spoken quietly, without particular emphasis. A certain restlessness swept the courtroom. The Judge warned the defendant that remarks of such a nature could only be interpreted as an effrontery. The Counsel for the Defense jumped up and objected to this reprimand, declaring it likely to produce an atmosphere prejudicial to his client, whose remark had, in fact, been completely misunderstood; and if his tone of voice had taken them aback, let the Court consider the misfortune that had just befallen his client and, as it were, thrown him off course, inevitably making it a matter of some difficulty for him to behave normally. Furthermore, his client had only meant to express his hope that the findings of this Court would also help him clarify his present circumstances, circumstances which he confessed himself no longer competent to understand, much less alter. Indeed, his client had signified to him in no uncertain terms—one might almost say implored him—that he expected his counsel to forego the introduction of obscure points of law in his defense. Or, to use his client's own words: "No legal rabbits out of questionable hats." And it was in the same spirit that his client renounced in advance—the Defense felt itself empowered to inform the Court of this now, at the beginning of the hearing—his right of further appeal. Whatever decision might be reached in his case had the prior acceptance of his client.

Be that as it may, the Judge remarked, even the present formulation by the defense seemed to contain something like indifference, intentionally flouted in the face of the Court. Let the defendant be advised not to continue in this vein. It would be taken for want of respect.

No, no, interrupted the defendant; that's not at all how it had been meant. Everything would be much simpler if the Court would only hasten to an unambiguous verdict of guilty. That was all he had meant to say. His court-appointed counsel had of course informed him that this was not possible, and that was why he had not objected; since admittedly he couldn't find anything to *defend,* or imagine what such a defense might amount to—for his Counsel had let it fall in conversation that he, the defendant, had no cause for worry since the Court would surely dismiss the case for lack of evidence.

At this, the Public Prosecutor grinned at the Defense Counsel, who shrugged his shoulders sadly.

But that, the defendant continued, would be the worst possible result.

The worst? asked the Judge, surprised.

Yes.

How can you call that the worst?

Such a result would give legal existence to uncertainty.

The worst for you?

For everyone, was the defendant's answer.

The Judge leafed through his papers and then remarked that he could not help sensing a certain doubt on the part of the defendant as to the Court's real competence in his case.

"No, no!" the defendant shouted once more, and this time with considerable excitement. "Where would that lead us?" He promised that he would do everything in his power to prevent the appearance of such a doubt. He understood how important to a court the awareness of its competence must be.

The Judge glanced at the Assessors and the Public Prosecutor. Then he said, "Very well. I am happy to see that you realize how important it is that your statements aid us in arriving at a just verdict."

The defendant expressed agreement with a slight nod of his head.

With that, the examination of evidence began. According to the defendant's deposition (whose validity was confirmed by several witnesses: a servant and a neighbor living two houses away who happened to have walked to the station for cigarettes), the beginning of the occurrence in question, which the defendant himself referred to by the mysterious words "departure into the uninsurable"—naturally, an expression totally meaningless before the law, but all the same to be used by the Court temporarily, that is, until the establishment of proven facts—the time of this so-called "departure" had to be somewhere between ten and midnight. Couldn't the defendant be more precise about the time?

No, since he hadn't looked at his watch. And time is of no consequence.

But for the Court it is. Now how could the defendant have concluded that his "departure" took place between ten and twelve if, as he now maintains, he hadn't looked at his watch?

His wife was in the habit of going to bed around ten, was the defendant's answer. He always stayed up two or three hours longer. The bedroom was on the second floor. That evening she'd come down again. And she hadn't yet undressed.

Undressed?

Changed into a long housecoat reaching to her feet, and of course a nightgown.

The Judge cleared his throat.

In any case, the defendant's wife came down from time to time?

No, never. Or if she did, it was always immediately after she'd gone up, and even then, only if she had left something behind.

How then did he explain that things happened differently this time?

He had not thought to explain it.

Well, how did he explain it now? There was irritation in the Judge's voice.

The defendant replied that there was nothing to explain. This was a simple fact requiring no explanation.

Hmmm! He hadn't been astonished by his wife's coming down at such an unusually late hour?

Astonished? The defendant thought a moment. It did seem to him now that he should have been astonished. Yet in fact he was certain that at the time he had not been astonished. There had simply been no opportunity.

What did he mean by that?

He was always astonished after the fact, as it were, after everything was over.

"Is it clear to you," asked the Judge, "how cynical your answer sounds?"

The defendant begged the Court's pardon if he had once more expressed himself clumsily. He had not meant anything cynical. Not at all! And after a short pause he added, "All the same . . . One doesn't have time for astonishment."

Very well. The Judge did not wish to become further involved in this discussion. Let the defendant continue with his account of the events of that evening. Even the most trivial particulars might be of the greatest consequence.

The defendant smiled. The Court took everything too seriously. The very nature of what did finally happen proves the total inconsequence of all that went before.

That may very well be, the Judge said with considerable sharpness; but the defendant should place in the hands of the Court and the Court alone all decision as to the importance of facts.

So that evening, too, he had returned from town around six?

Yes, like any day except Saturday, the defendant affirmed. He had always taken the 5:25 from the Central Station. At five minutes to six it reached the suburban station, and that's eight minutes from home.

Hmmm, yes. That agrees with the deposition of witnesses. And indeed the defendant had left his office that day too a little past five, as his assistant and the other employees had testified. So, without a stop from office to house? His business was insurance, wasn't it? And what sort of insurance did he handle?

Every imaginable variety of insurance: life, accident, liability, fire, theft, transportation, and so on . . .

Had anything unusual occurred that day?

Anything unusual?

Yes, an unusually complicated or disturbing business transaction, for example?

No, nothing like that. It was an ordinary business day.

"Your agency has a good reputation," the Judge remarked in passing, more to the public than to the defendant. "You are an honest broker and a dependable adviser—to that both insurers and insured agree."

"All that is over now," remarked the defendant with a smile as he, too, turned to the courtroom.

"If you please," warned the Judge, "such observations are out of place here."

At this point the Prosecutor interrupted. "Tell me, defendant, isn't it true, as I see here, that four, no, five years ago you insured your life for 50,000 marks, in favor of your wife? Was there any *particular* reason for this policy at the time you took it out?"

The defendant complained that he did not understand the question.

"Did you feel at the time that some misfortune might soon overtake you? Something might have occurred which made you stop and think . . . It needn't have been that your life was actually in danger."

No, his life was always, every minute, in the same danger.

"Did your wife know about this life insurance?"

Yes, of course. Her knowing about it could almost be said to be more important than the insurance itself.

"Did anyone else know about it?"

The insurance company, of course, and the Internal Revenue. Policies of this kind have to be declared on one's tax form. Oh, and his agency's accountant knew all about it because of the payment of the premiums. Perhaps his bank, too.

"Yes, quite right. But that isn't at all what I meant.

What I'm driving at is whether *someone else* knew about your life insurance. A friend, for instance."

The defendant explained that he had no friends.

"All right then, an acquaintance. Perhaps your wife mentioned the policy to someone."

No, why should she have done that?

"In passing. Let me give you an example. A friend —or let us say an acquaintance—of your wife's complains that her husband has done nothing to provide for her. Things like that do happen. So your wife tells her that you have taken out a policy in her favor. She may even say it in the hope of sending you and your agency some business."

No, his wife never meddled in his business. That had not been her way, and if the Prosecutor had only known her, the suspicion would not have occurred to him.

"Suspicion? Who said anything about suspicion? But let's leave this question. Wouldn't you say that 50,000 marks is an unusually large amount?"

That all depends, was the defendant's reply. It is all a question of whether one is in a position to pay the premiums. Five years ago, as a matter of fact, the premiums were quite high for his income, but business had taken such a turn for the better that the premiums were no longer a hardship.

"All the same, 50,000 marks is a considerable sum."

It only appeared so. One should not be taken in by appearances. He had figured it all out at the time;

with the money paid out by the insurance company, plus any interest accruing from the unused portion, his wife could live in ease for twelve or at the most fifteen years—assuming she had no other source of income. So 50,000 marks turns out not to be so much after all, especially as it's likely his wife would out-live him by more than fifteen years.

"So you count on your immediate, or let us say proximate, demise?"

Certainly. Night and day. Hourly.

"Why?"

It would be frivolous not to.

"Are you speaking as an insurance agent?"

The defendant smiled. No, it would hardly do for an insurance agent to talk like that. And into the bargain, should war or inflation ensue, all these calculations became purely illusory. In reality there was no "security"—in his line of business, one was only too aware of this. But of course that, too, was something one didn't tell one's clients. As for his own case, he had chosen this particular sum because it conjured up an impression of security. And that is all one can attain. And it's more or less a—prolongation.

"Prolongation?" the Prosecutor asked without a pause. "What did you mean to prolong?"

The inevitable . . . Whatever you want to call that something which no insurance covers.

"Hmmm. I understand. And just one more question, please. In whose favor is this policy?"

How's that? The only beneficiary was his wife.

"Yes, of course. But supposing she were no longer living . . ."

"Do you know for a certainty?" the defendant asked in terror.

"I was only supposing . . ."

"That is one thing you dare not suppose," the defendant answered angrily.

The Judge wanted to intervene, but the Prosecutor warned him off with a nod.

"Pardon me for expressing myself so clumsily," he said. "I only meant this. Who would you substitute as beneficiary, were your wife to predecease you—which might occur quite naturally."

Such an eventuality had never even entered into his deliberations. It was altogether too farfetched. Of course the sum would be paid out to him on his reaching the age of sixty. But that was still a long way off and his chance of reaching such an age seemed quite slim. Once more the defendant smiled, as if to say this all struck him as funny.

"Why so pessimistic?" the Prosecutor asked. "I have every intention of reaching sixty and then some."

The defendant regarded the Prosecutor closely for a moment, then nodded and said: "In that case, such a policy would hardly be right for you."

The public laughed. Before the Judge could call them to order, the Prosecutor was speaking again.

"Thank you for the advice. But let's return to the business at hand. Please tell me, who would you substitute as beneficiary in the event that your wife predeceased you?"

He simply *wouldn't*. If the policy no longer had a purpose, he'd just leave it as is.

"In that case, your wife's heirs very probably have a legitimate claim."

"My wife's heirs?" The defendant was taken aback. Yes, indeed, his wife did have a brother and a sister, both married, both with children. "Oh, well, what's the difference?" But he found it most unpleasant to discuss the death of his wife here. It seemed to him something—impermissible.

"And it is not impossible that your own heirs would have to be taken into consideration," the Prosecutor continued.

His heirs! The defendant replied with the greatest conviction that he had no heirs.

"Oh, yes! For instance, there's your mother. It's she who's your next of kin."

The defendant was visibly frightened. For a moment he seemed to be losing his grip on himself. He was swiftly in control again, however; and only the absolutely calm tone of voice in which he answered betrayed his uncertainty. He said, "My mother has means of her own and is financially independent. The Court can appraise itself of the truth of my statement any time it wishes. Thus she is not in the position of having to count on my death to pay her bills."

The Judge put an end to this argument. The question of the defendant's heirs was only of hypothetical interest. Did the Prosecutor intend to put further questions?

"Yes, but only one more. Tell us, defendant, did you also insure your wife?"

No, why should he have done that?

At this juncture the Defense intervened. Counsel felt that this was the moment to remark that his client not only had named his wife beneficiary in the event of his death, but over and above that, years before he had put all his property in her name—their house, for instance. Such forethought and trust as the defendant demonstrated in this respect were surely exemplary.

The remark of the Defense would be duly noted by the Court—and the Prosecution thanked him. The interpretation of these facts, however, he would reserve for a future time.

The defendant interjected that all this was getting far too involved. The situation was really much simpler. Possessions meant nothing to him, so he had burdened his wife with them. And as for insurance: it happens very seldom that a husband insures his wife. Reaping a profit from an accident to his wife is repugnant to a man, however legal and irreproachable this profit may be. And besides, the percentage of women who outlive their husbands is far greater than the other way around . . . Statistics don't lie. Thus it is only natural that a man consider the probability of his death, if only to give his wife some feeling of security.

"A security, however, in which you yourself do not happen to believe," observed the Prosecution.

But that was hardly the question at the moment. His Honor had just now been kind enough to qualify him as "dependable." And really, what had there been for him, the defendant, to be, if not dependable? As long as one had to deal with matters one could not possibly believe in, dependability alone offered a chance of gaining the upper hand. It was a question, after all, of what his wife believed; he had tried to ease the present for her by removing, or at least seeming to remove, all concern for the future.

"In this you do not seem to have succeeded." There was malice in the Prosecutor's voice.

"It never succeeds for more than seconds at a time," the defendant admitted.

The Judge tapped on the table with his pencil and warned all parties concerned to avoid digressions that could confuse the course of the hearing unnecessarily. First of all, in point of fact, there is this matter of reconstructing the events of that day and of the hours immediately preceding this so-called "departure into the uninsurable."

During the day, while in his office, had the defendant received a telephone call from his wife?

Yes.

Was this a usual occurrence?

Yes, daily, as a matter of fact.

Was there any particular reason for these calls?

They were most often occasioned by her needing something which he must buy in town as it wasn't to be had in the suburbs.

Why hadn't his wife asked him before he left home in the morning?

She hadn't thought of it yet. Or she had noticed the lack during the course of the day. Sometimes she did mention it to him in the morning, and then called later to remind him.

Could he remember what it was his wife had asked him for that day?

N-no . . . Why, yes. If he recalled rightly, it was those coffee filters she wanted. A particular size that the neighborhood store never carried. He believed they were number 102, but he might be mistaken.

The Judge verified this answer. A package containing two cartons of filters had been found. It had never been opened.

His wife probably wouldn't have had time for that.

Hmm. That was possible, of course.

The Prosecution asked for the floor and put the following question: "How are we to explain, then, that in a kitchen cabinet we found seven cartons of these filters, still unopened; and an eighth carton besides, partially empty but with about twenty filters still in it?"

The defendant smiled as though to himself. Well, that was a real cache, wasn't it; how would he have known about it—snooping in kitchen cabinets had never been his habit. But even if he had come across it, he would have gone on behaving as though the purchase of new filters were an absolute necessity. He had realized, of course, that their consumption of filters was phenomenal.

"You mean you never discussed this with your wife?"

No, it was better not to.

"Thank you!" said the Prosecutor.

The Defense Counsel was about to object but was prevented by the Judge, who wanted to know if, in other words, these filters had been only a pretext.

Yes. The defendant acknowledged that they were —and everything else.

Everything else? What did he mean by that?

He meant this whole way of life. But no one must get wind of that. It would only upset those involved, without doing anyone else any good. Especially in the case of such trivia as those unnecessary filters; best not to let even a mention of them reach the surface when a mere mention risks bringing down the whole edifice, and before its time. Trivia—nothing's more dangerous.

How's that? Why trivia in particular?

Probably because there is so much trivia that no one can keep track of it all. Indeed, just when one is least prepared, trivia let insecurity become apparent.

Had his wife any reason to be unsure of him?

"Of *me?*" the defendant exclaimed, surprised.

All right, the Judge continued after a moment. Those filters, and the other errands, were nothing but a pretext for his wife to call him. In reality, she wanted to ascertain whether he was in his office or not.

In his office? What did this have to do with his office? Offices, too, are only pretexts.

Very well, let's not argue. We'll only entangle ourselves in more pretexts.

Yes, precisely, the defendant agreed.

Yet he must have had to visit his clients often? the Prosecutor asked—obviously to help out the Judge.

Naturally. In his line of business there was no other way. Other than personal contact, he meant. He had been on the go almost every day.

And what would have happened if his wife had called while he was out?

Usually he informed her of his appointments for the day. If not, he always left address and phone number in his office, so that if necessary his wife could reach him.

And had his wife actually called him in clients' homes or offices?

Yes, that too happened.

Didn't he find this embarrassing?

Why?

His clients must have wondered why.

They probably thought his wife helped him in his business and had some important news of a business nature which couldn't wait. What else could they have thought? As for him, he was aware of the possibility that his wife might have need to hear his voice; although, as had already been observed, he kept his wife informed as nearly as possible of his every step.

As nearly as possible?

Yes, as nearly as possible. Because here we are concerned with pretexts, with events that can be discussed and decided upon, whereas with the reality that sneaks in behind us we have no warning but an intuition, night or day. To talk about such things in the same breath as these old reliable pretexts would be an unworthy deception.

Had such unexpected "incidents," so to speak, occurred often enough to give his wife reasonable grounds to fear their repetition?

Unexpected? It had been anything but "unexpected"! On the contrary, it had been expected, and as he had already emphasized, day and night. And there lay the reason for his wife's calling him all the time. To make sure he was there still—or if the time had come. Of course one cannot ask such a question point-blank; it isn't done; one reason why it isn't is due directly to their not knowing—neither he nor his wife—precisely *what* was to be expected. In such a situation those filters supplied appropriate means . . .

To avoid the possibility of their simply talking past each other, said the Prosecutor, he was going to ask a very personal question: the defendant had a very jealous wife?

If by that the Prosecution meant that the fear existed that he, the defendant, might fall prey to another woman, then of course the answer was yes, like any other woman, his wife feared that too. And as for him, he had never considered himself "proof against seduction." Perhaps this was truer of him than of most men, and his wife felt it.

He expressed himself in a remarkably cautious manner . . . Had his wife a *definite* reason for feeling this? Or, more precisely, did his wife have reason to expect a repetition of a particular case?

But all women have! If nothing else, they have their own "case" as an example, and fear its repetition with another.

And how are we to take that?

Women, girls are on the loose in the streets, stairways, railroad stations. Men's thoughts and men's desires are on the loose too in those very places, and men's fatigue . . . Occasionally, one of the first runs into one of the second—oh, without either of them intending it. They stumble and stand in confrontation for a second, as they cannot yield to right or left, and as they are afraid to pass through each other (because it might hurt), they pretend they have found the end of their road.

Very well, but the Prosecution wanted to know how the defendant's wife felt about all this.

All what?

All this, this "standing in confrontation for a second," as the defendant called it.

But *he* never had, he had always passed straight through!

Did he intend that as a euphemism for fleeting erotic experiences?

As far as he knew, this expression which the Prosecution had just used meant something more concrete, indeed something actionable; something too, against which certain forms of insurance were available. No, he had not meant that, and it was unimportant besides.

Well then, what had he meant by "pass through"?

Pass through? The defendant shrugged his shoulders helplessly. What on earth required further explanation? One just *passes through,* and then . . . One could never be sure, though, that a scent wouldn't linger with him, perhaps a few minutes, perhaps all his life. One would not even be able to smell it oneself because it would become one's own scent. Or perhaps a little patch of skin was rubbed off . . . Not literally, not something one could treat with a salve or cover with a Band-Aid. He was speaking figuratively, yet all the same, the skin grows thinner and thinner and another can notice it . . .

Aha! His wife had noticed it?

A woman cannot conceive of a man existing without one of them; and this question hadn't been settled yet one way or the other, though most religions insist it has. It's only natural that religions and women disagree. Women think something like this: If it isn't me, it must be some other *woman*. And no matter how much they may suffer at that thought, their suffering at least has a real object, so it's bearable; whereas the other possibility would mean final dismay and annihilation for them; therefore they don't even dare entertain it.

Aha! the Prosecutor cried once more. In other words, the defendant believed that his wife would have preferred to have thought him unfaithful?

The Defense tried to object, but his client waved him aside. Worry and anger, he said, might have supplied her with a sort of assurance. "But," he added, "this was something I had no intention of providing for her."

"And why is that?" interjected the Prosecutor hastily.

"I have always resisted putting off a solution to a problem at the expense of others. And in any case, I don't wish to use my wife, or anyone else's, as a means of evading the problem."

"I don't follow you completely. What problem are you talking about?"

"The one we've been talking about all along! What you, sir, have called 'the unexpected,' although that's surely a misnomer, since all of us do expect it."

"Could you be more explicit?"

"It could be described as that against which *there is no insurance.*"

Laughter in the Court. The Judge warned the public not to disturb the hearing.

The defendant turned to the public with a pained expression and shouted: "I did not intend that as a joke!" For this he received a reprimand.

After quiet had been reestablished, the Judge said: "Mr. Attorney, I believe we could now move on to . . ."

"If you please, one more question before we leave this subject," said the Prosecutor. And turning to the defendant: "By 'that against which we cannot be insured,' do you mean death?"

"Death? Of course one can be insured against that. I mean life."

"How's that? And your wife in all probability departed this life!"

"Who says so?" This question was asked so sharply, so clearly that all who heard it held their breaths for an instant. "And if you believe you possess proof, out with it! Why are we here? Why are you putting me and the Court through all this? It's a sheer waste of time! Because if the situation really is as you dare to imply, then I've *failed*. And a failure is always guilty. No long legal hassle is required."

The Judge intended to reprimand the defendant a second time for this unheard-of outburst against the Court, but the Prosecution was quicker and got in ahead of him. "Tell me, defendant, are you a religious man?"

That could be. He had never worried his head about it.

"How's that?"

He had never had the time. He hadn't been in a church since his confirmation.

"Would you, if this Court brings an indictment, take an oath 'by God'?"

Yes, why not?

"That is hardly an answer."

What answer was expected of him then? Hadn't he promised, from the beginning, to present no difficulties; indeed, to do all he could to help the Court? And if justice were aided by his swearing "by God," why would the Prosecution suppose that he would refuse?

The Defense jumped up. "I object, your Honor! The insinuations of the Prosecution have no object but the creation of an atmosphere prejudicial to my client."

"Objection sustained," ruled the Judge. "This is no place to argue theology. The Court's task is this and this alone: to determine a woman's fate and to decide the defendant's responsibility. Once more I implore the parties concerned not to digress from this subject."

All the same, the Prosecution wanted to return to this business of the daily phone calls. "You admit, defendant, that you knew for certain that these calls were a pretext for your wife for . . . for . . ."

"For hearing my voice." The defendant completed the Prosecutor's sentence.

"Aha! Good! So she wanted to hear your voice. And in your opinion this sufficed to give your wife the security she so obviously lacked?"

"That all depends . . . For an hour perhaps; perhaps through the afternoon. Even till a new day dawned. In other words, as long as she could believe in it."

"So, although you were aware that your wife needed to hear your voice to continue to believe in you, you never—the testimony of all witnesses agrees in this—you never thought it proper to call her yourself?"

"No, I never did."

"Thank you. That is enough."

Again the Defense would have liked to object to the biased methods of the Prosecution. But the defendant himself waved this aside. He said that although one had to be there when the call came, nothing could be more wrong-headed than calling oneself. That would mean acknowledging the other's insecurity far too conspicuously, and only increase the other's lack of independence. The doctor never tells a patient that his disease is incurable; he's always given a chance. Indeed, this is the only chance one has of transcending the incurable. His wife would have thought: Why did he call? What's the matter with him? Perhaps the time has come? Yes, his calling might actually have been interpreted as a warning. Or as a threat even. No, no one should allow himself to do a thing like that! And besides, even in business such tactics would be wrong. One never talked to a client too much about death and accidents; that would only scare him off. Fear is a poor argument in business. No sooner has one created it than it gets the upper hand and the client begins to think: "Why even bother to plan ahead? Putting up a fight is useless. It's all a fraud. No one profits but the insurance companies, except the government perhaps, since it's always glad to learn of another case where it won't need to pay social security." And more of the same . . . How much better to explain to the client that once he's insured he will not be worrying day and night about his dependants' future; that he'll sleep better, he'll actually lengthen his life and increase his vitality.

"We did not interrupt your detailed exposition," said the Judge, "because this Court must gain insight into your odd modes of thought. Yet I believe I am not speaking only for myself, but expressing the feelings of all those present, when I tell you that it strikes us as uncommonly strange that you always speak of yourself as though for your wife you were nothing more than some sort of insurance."

But that's just how it was! cried the defendant. Not as money or as property, of course, but insurance in the abstract. That was the terrible thing. And that both parties feel how easily tempted they might be to commit insurance fraud. It was here that the closest scrutiny was necessary. No deception seemed more cunning than the attempt to claim absolute security for something which one knows, or ought to know, is highly undependable, something possessed even of the little validity it has under certain conditions only, and those conditions themselves resting on the most provisional of agreements.

"You consider the relationship between a man and his wife a provisional agreement?" the Prosecution suddenly interrupted.

"Not the relationship, but its outcome: what we call a blind alley."

"Marriage then, if I get your meaning."

"Not only marriage. Everything!"

"Everything?"

"If you will permit me to say so, Mr. Attorney, I do not comprehend how you can persist in these questions."

"Because all of us, if I am not mistaken, think in much more absolute terms about the validity of marriage and what you call 'everything'!" the Prosecutor answered triumphantly.

"Yes, you are right," replied the defendant with concern, "and I am aware of this. And for this very reason you should be more careful. In the interests of your own point of view, you should avoid anything likely to awaken *doubt,* and that is precisely the outcome of such questions. All these things—and you know this as well as I do—enjoy their validity only so long as all of us assembled here in this chamber are willing to think about them in such absolute terms, as you put it, that calling them in question would never cross our minds. And I—you will forgive me for repeating this—declared in the beginning my willingness to recognize this absolute validity which the Court finds so essential."

Before the Judge could intervene, the Defense asked for the floor. For his part, he begged the Court's pardon for his client's tone and manner, improper in a courtroom, of carrying on his argument with the Prosecution. But the whole responsibility lay with the Prosecutor's indefensible manner of discriminating against the defendant psychologically, a plan of attack for which there was obviously no excuse but the Prosecution's apparent lack of any concrete evidence that would justify his bringing action. Small wonder that his client, offended by such shameful tactics, should be driven to defend himself with odd-sounding answers that everyone was ready to admit were antisocial. If the Court would have the goodness to take this into consideration . . .

The Court had that goodness. Once more the Judge gathered up the various threads of the case.

So the defendant had returned home that evening around six, as on any other evening. Had he noticed anything unusual as he came in the door? In his wife's behavior perhaps, as she greeted him? Or later, for that matter?

No, why? What could there have been for him to notice? His wife had met him at the door with a kiss, as usual. Then she asked if there had been a great deal to do or if anything unpleasant had happened at the office. She did so every evening, so this could not be considered unusual. And then they had changed the subject. Gone on to talk about the repair man, he believed, who was supposed to come fix the float in the toilet tank. And then they must have talked about whether or not they should order more coal for the winter, as his wife had heard that the price was going to go up. Oh, and also about a letter that had arrived that day from his mother—it was on his desk.

And what did it say, the Judge wanted to know.

Nothing, really. He had torn it up immediately.

Why?

He hadn't opened the letter until after dinner and had handed it to his wife right away. So that she wouldn't think it contained anything unpleasant. And then he had torn it up.

Yes, but why had he torn it up immediately?

Oh, he'd been in the habit of doing that since he was a boy.

Did the letter contain anything that might have annoyed either his wife or him?

Letters always contain something annoying—one realized that just seeing them lying there unopened. But this letter didn't contain more than the usual nonsense relatives write one another. The weather, illnesses, visits, other relatives. This time it had been a sort of bread-and-butter letter. His mother had just celebrated her seventy-second birthday, and his wife had sent a present.

All the less reason, the Judge thought, for anyone to tear it up immediately.

Into little pieces.

Why, for God's sake?

He always did, except of course with business letters.

Did he do it to avoid piling up useless paper?

That too, of course, but principally because in certain situations collecting letters can be dangerous.

Dangerous? How?

When the letter arrives, one reads it and finds nothing unsettling in it, and perhaps there's nothing there that ought to bother one. Yet years later, re-reading a letter by chance, one may feel somehow the news it contained was unsettling—though it's possible of course that this has to do with one's way of reading. At all costs, one should avoid exposing one-self to such an eventuality.

Had he also torn up all his wife's letters?

Yes, hers in particular.

How's that?

There had never been many of them. He and his wife had seldom been apart. Once or twice he'd had to go on a business trip alone, and once she had taken a vacation when his business couldn't spare him. Oh, and in the beginning, too, they had exchanged some letters. That was all.

Would he please explain what it was about his wife's letters that had made him say "Hers in particu-lar" with reference to tearing up letters?

It was to prevent them from ever falling into her hands again; she might have felt embarrassed on re-reading them, or might have felt melancholy. With-out reasonable grounds, of course, but reading old letters does that. If one reads them, one has to be pre-pared for such mortal melancholy. No, one must never look back. One should immediately place a soundproof barrier between oneself and one's every yesterday. No one is strong enough to hear a voice from the past and not feel impelled to turn around, and whoever does so will stumble, lose his way, and then he is almost certainly forever lost. "For our past is a horror and stronger than the urge to go on."

"I have never heard of such curious security meas-ures," the Judge exclaimed.

And the Prosecutor, who had been readying his ambush, asked, "Are you aware of the fact, defendant, that in contrast to your practice, your wife had arranged all your letters chronologically and that they were found tied with a ribbon in her desk?"

He had been afraid of that, but what could he do? He only hoped that his wife had never reread them. Did the Prosecution feel that his wife had done so?

"In the police report," the Prosecutor admitted, "it is stated that the bundle of letters tied up in a yellow ribbon did not appear to have been touched for some time."

The defendant heaved a sigh of relief.

"You have been married seven years?" asked the Judge.

"Yes."

"Did you treat your wife like this from the very beginning?"

The defendant did not answer. He did not appear to have understood the Judge's question.

"I mean, these security measures which seem so strange to us. Almost as though she were an enemy."

"Security measures? But not against my wife!"

"Whom then?"

The defendant hesitated and glanced helplessly from the Judge to the Assessors. Hadn't he explained all this already? he asked finally.

"Very well. Enough of this. Let's have no more of your 'uninsurable,' though! But there is another question which you may be able to answer for us. Is there any particular reason why your marriage remained childless for so long? It is my duty, by the way, to caution you that you are under no obligation to answer. And if you prefer, or consider it essential, I am prepared to have the court cleared."

This question seemed to amuse the defendant. Why clear the court? It was no secret. It was terribly simple. His wife and he, before they married, had agreed that under no circumstances would they have children.

"Under no circumstances?"

"Exactly."

"How old was your wife when you married?" asked the Prosecutor.

She had been twenty-six; he, thirty-two.

"In the event that your wife had become pregnant, you would have considered medical intervention?" the Prosecution probed.

That . . . That . . . The question disturbed the defendant. Yes, perhaps, but he had never really considered the possibility, and the situation had never come up. And besides, there was a law against it. In all probability he would have let his wife decide.

"Why did you marry at all if you had decided beforehand that you did not want children?"

Once again the defendant looked helplessly around him; this time he even looked out into the courtroom, as though the spectators might have some support to offer.

At this point the Defense intervened. He couldn't help asking the Prosecutor if he had ever heard of a man marrying for love. And he, in his role of counsel for the defense, had never come across a law forbidding childless marriages.

The law took the natural intentions of the parties to a marriage into consideration, the Prosecutor answered, in that it recognized, yes recognized, not just allowed, intentional childlessness, you might almost call it criminal childlessness, as grounds for divorce. "But since the Defense has spoken of love," the Prosecutor continued somewhat louder, "let me ask if loving a woman does not include or even presuppose the desire to have children by her? That, at any rate, is my understanding, and I flatter myself that it jibes with the generally held definition of love, so much so that no legal expression of it has ever been deemed necessary."

The Judge wished to know if the Prosecution insisted on continuing in this vein.

"Yes, I do, in order to give the Court some notion of this young woman's martyrdom, upon which she entered out of love—yes, there was surely love on her side—but without a thought to the far-reaching consequences of agreeing to this unnatural and inhuman refusal of children. This martyrdom, which lasted so many years, could only lead to a tragic conclusion."

An excited argument between the Defense and the Prosecution broke out at this point, but it does not need recapitulation here. The Defense protested most of all against the use of the words "martyrdom" and "tragic conclusion"—where was the proof? These words were designed simply to prejudice his client's case. The Prosecution, on the other hand, obliged them with high-sounding phrases, which remained without effect, however, against the irony of the Defense and the defendant's silent, astonished manner of listening to all this. Finally, the Judge put an end to this exchange.

Turning to the defendant, he desired to know whether there had been any particular reason for entering upon this agreement, odd as it seemed, before the marriage? Had there perhaps been financial grounds?

No, it had nothing to do with money, the defendant wanted to emphasize that. Even then, he had been in a position to support a family.

"Moreover," said the Judge. "I believe I am correct in supposing that neither your health nor your wife's was at fault. Or did you entertain doubts on this account?"

No, they had both been sound as a bell to the very end, the defendant assured him. But they weren't the world's only childless couple. Why was he singled out for suspicion of some special motive?

The Court, indeed, suspected him of some special motive, he was right about that. The Court went so far as to expect to shed some light on the whole business as a result of uncovering this particular motivation.

He would rather not answer.

Of course he could refuse to answer. It was his right.

Oh no, that sounded far too solemn and grand. It wasn't as if there were anything to hide; let the Court rest assured of that. It was just that he was afraid he'd be misunderstood, he already had been misunderstood all too often . . . It would only make trouble.

Let him speak all the same, the Judge demanded.

The mistake . . . No, that's not it, either. He begged the Court's pardon, and especially the Prosecution's . . . Their difference was most clearly expressed in the word "natural," which the Prosecution had used.

Well, did he feel that children or a desire for children was *un*natural?

No, not in the least! He felt it was very natural, even *terribly* natural; yes, that was it.

And?

How's that? There's no "and"! That was the whole thing in a nutshell . . .

There was no possibility that he might make himself clearer?

Yes, but then he would surely be called to order. Children are a link with the past!

"With the past!" the Judge couldn't help exclaiming.

Yes, it's only natural.

"All of us here are of the opinion that children constitute a step forward, something to come."

The defendant smiled sadly. Yes, that too was only —natural. Into lock-step with nature, since there was no other way. A sort of relapse. And if the Court would allow it, without anger, a very provisional form of insurance.

The Judge waved aside any reaction from the Prosecution as well as from the public. "Were your wife's ideas the same as yours?" he asked the defendant.

Of course he couldn't say for sure; this was a matter only for conjecture. What a person really thought on any subject depended so very much on the passing mood, for women more than for men; and so it happens that the world and the lives of individuals are driven by moods, mostly into blind alleys. To think this through to its conclusion was hard enough for a man, and for a woman it was so dreadful that any man, seeing it, would feel so helpless that he would do anything, even if it was the wrong thing, to help his wife out of such a mood, even if in the act she would be dragged even further into the deadly circuit.

What "deadly circuit"?

"You know those old-fashioned revolving eleva-
tors one still finds in some places? At some point,
one jumped in with the intention of jumping out
at some floor or other. That was one's intention.
One must have known why exactly, and where one
wanted to go. In any event, *up!* Everything seemed
very simple. But all that was forgotten long ago; try as
one will, one cannot remember, and nothing else
seems to make any sense either. All one can think is:
'If only I hadn't jumped into this elevator! What
on earth tempted me to do it?' For, against all
reasonable expectations, it turns out that the elevator is moving up too fast for anyone to dare get out
again. This realization is so sudden that at first one
isn't even afraid. When one got in, it certainly wasn't
noticeable, or one certainly wouldn't have got in.
There are stairs, too, you know . . . They are certainly safer. But how did it happen? Perhaps a gov-
ernor suddenly broke. Or the superintendent acceler-
ated the mechanism to test something. But in that
case he should have put up a sign: WARNING DO NOT
USE CLOSED FOR REPAIRS. At this point, though, it no
longer matters who's responsible. The speed at which
one is being carried up has reached such a pitch, the
floors just flit by. If one were to jump out now, one
would probably be crushed between the floor of the
car and the ceiling of the floor he'd chosen. Of course,
in the interests of safety the footboards had been installed so that they would spring up, but who was

going to trust to that? And for that reason one thinks it would be far better to go right on over the roof; jumping out is easier on the way down. Because of the speed, one has to reckon with the possibility of being dumped on the floor, but even so, it's better than being crushed between elevator and ceiling. And so the mind quiets down as one goes over the roof, past the great wheel dripping with black grease. Because of the skylight, all this stands out quite vividly. And when one has passed the divide and begun one's descent, then one resolves: 'Now's the time!' But the top floors make one feel that one's insufficiently prepared. Why the hurry? There are so many floors still to come. One stands ready, the whole body tensed, and when the next floor approaches, one sticks out a foot by way of a trial. But at the last minute one pulls it back; it's better to wait for a lower floor. And this way one descends further and further. 'Self-possession is the order of the day!' one thinks, and why not go through the cellar anyway? There's an enamel plaque in the elevator that says you can go through the cellar safely. *Safely!* You don't say! In other words, there must be danger, or they wouldn't mention it. But certainly no danger as long as you stay in the elevator. This is consoling as one heads through the cellar, where total darkness reigns. The machinery cracks like gouty joints. There it's only a question of keeping still. And before you know it, up again! The same old tour you had before

. . . The cycle repeated. It's pretty bad. And how long is it going to go on? Wouldn't it be better to jump out and make a future, no matter what? Now, this revolving without a future is . . . It's all very well for someone who has the terra firma of a floor un-der his feet to ask: 'Well, why not step out?' From his standpoint, there's no way to gauge the speed of the elevator, and even less to judge what it takes to make the necessary decision. It all looks perfectly normal to him, and he may even believe the whole thing's a joke because one keeps grimacing. And how is one to answer? How can anyone else know what trouble one is in? Just call back: 'In a minute, in a minute!' Or 'I'm getting out at the next floor.' And that wouldn't really be a lie, as one really does intend to get out there. Nothing one would rather do! It's the right an-swer. Only after one knows the whole circuit, is it no longer right. Naturally, when he hears that no one has jumped out, the person standing outside will think, 'Hold on, there. He was lying . . . He was just trying to talk his way out.' If only one could *talk* one's way out of this! You'll hear that some do get out: they lose their judgment, dizzied by the merci-less cycle. For example, if there's a good-looking girl standing out on the landing, or just one who looks good as she whizzes by, one risks the jump. What funny motions one makes, trying to regain one's bal-ance. It's hard to hold back laughter . . . But one believes at last one has firm ground under one's feet;

that one's survived the elevator's circling. Every so often, one hears it rasp and crack behind one's back, but now one has this girl to hold tight. A short story! A limited success! A small-scale war! A private religion! So the girl, too, becomes part of the cycle, and she, too, is crushed. And she would not have it otherwise.

"'No! No! No!' one would like to shout. Perhaps someone will hear and run down the steps three at a time to the superintendent to make him stop the machinery.

"But no one shouts. Forgive me, gentlemen. One cannot shout, it's like a bad dream. And to what end would one disturb the good people who live on their solid floors? One has to find out how one's to get through it without crying out for help."

It would be difficult to say why the Judge, instead of stopping the defendant, allowed him to tell his overly long and certainly irrelevant parable to the very end. However, there was no denying that the defendant knew how to tell a story. In the courtroom you could have heard a pin drop; the public listened as if enchanted. It seemed that what the defendant called "a bad dream" had taken hold of all of them. The Prosecution alone seemed untouched, and he brought the hearing back to reality.

"Did you cherish the wish to have no children whatever," he asked, "or simply none with this particular woman, your wife?"

This question came as a surprise to everyone, after what had gone before. No one was able to understand its purpose, the defendant least of all. He didn't know what to say.

"To formulate my question more precisely," the Prosecution said after waiting longer than necessary, "did your wife possibly exercise a sort of physical repulsion upon you, or vice versa?"

The defendant considered the Prosecutor with interest, examining him from head to foot without saying a word, but clearly without malice; no, rather as if attempting to discover what could have made him believe it necessary to ask a question like that. Finally, the attorney reacted: "Well?"

"Don't children come into the world in spite of this 'physical repulsion,' as you call it?" the defendant asked, smiling slightly.

"That's no answer."

"No, perhaps it isn't. I only wanted to make people forget a question which I believe you asked inadvertently."

Before the Prosecutor could show how outraged he was, the Defense jumped up, doubtless to demand that the Judge put a stop to this inquisition. But the Defense, too, was prevented from speaking by a wave of his client's hand.

"No, thank you very much, Mr. Counsel, it isn't a question of the public. Even if the public were removed, I would not be in a position to answer the

Prosecution's question. This question belongs among
those which are impermissible. Just that word 'physical'—pardon, your Honor; this is my wife we are talking about—seems impermissible. It is quite possible
that in juridical usage this word has a different sense,
but to me it only means the uncovering of our nakedness. I have to protect myself from that. And besides,
the Court has nothing to gain by my answering; on
the contrary, it would mean that the Court had over-
stepped the bounds of its competence into a region
in which the laws have no validity. May I ask the
Prosecutor a question?"

"Certainly."

"Have you ever heard a woman crying in the next
room?"

"Well, what if I have? Why this question?"

"My question is meant as an answer."

"How? Did your wife cry a great deal?"

"Any woman at all, Mr. Attorney."

"I cannot comprehend your meaning."

"And by that I see for certain that you never have.
Your Honor, I promised to do my best to aid this
Court. For that reason I will say what I feel the absence of my wife compels me to say!" The defendant
examined the public rapidly, row by row, as though
he once more needed to convince himself that his
wife wasn't really present. Involuntarily, the eyes of
all the officials searched the courtroom, too. The public seemed to hold its breath. At length the defend-

ant continued: "To be sure, from the very beginning we were ashamed of our inhumanity."

"What do you mean by inhumanity?" asked the Judge.

"What we were just talking about, all that's physical."

"You said 'we'?"

"I said 'we.'"

"And from the very beginning?"

"From the very beginning. That's how it was."

The Judge seemed disposed after this soft but definite "That's how it was" to leave this line of questioning, but the Prosecution was not yet satisfied. He asked the defendant if he could tell, in a few words, how he came to know his wife.

"In a few words?" the defendant repeated.

The Judge asked the Prosecution if it considered such a digression absolutely necessary.

Yes, the Prosecutor insisted upon the Court's arriving at a clear picture of the past. So the Judge requested the defendant to be as brief as possible.

The defendant stated that he had known his wife from the time she was a child. And later as a young girl. During summer vacations. One summer vacation after another, for years and years. Then for a long time he'd neither seen her nor heard from her. Nor had they written to each other. She had been sent to boarding school, to a convent where the Sisters were very strict. Her parents had sent her there because

48

they wished her to have a better education. And he,
too, had studied and then stopped—lack of money,
and other reasons—and tried this and that, until he
had reached the end of his tether. He had walked to
the station and bought a ticket. Third class, local
train. To go get his wife . . . He hadn't had enough
money for the express, that's why. He had traveled
the whole night through, from around eight in the
evening until after ten the next morning. The church
bells had been ringing when he arrived, so it must
have been Sunday. And he had been the only person
to get out there. Everyone else had already gotten
out, one by one. The train had stopped at every little
station.

The Prosecution wanted to know why he went
into such detail about the local.

Because he had traveled the whole night through,
and the sound was still in his ears, the rhythm of the
wheels, the puffing of the engine, the groans of the
couplings. He had been afraid that his car would
break loose and roll back to where he'd started. They
had been very old cars. And the smell, too, was still
in his nostrils, of rust and metal and dirt and sweat.
He had been awfully hungry and other passengers
had had their bread and fruit, especially apples, and
these had had a smell. But the train hadn't been very
full, and in the end it was empty, him alone. When
he got out, he had been stiff, and dizzy at first. It had
been raining a little, a very little really, and more of

a mist than rain, and even that stopped after a while and then the sun peeked through here and there. But it had been very pale and hesitant. And he too, he looked very pale from his tiring journey—so people told him.

What people?

Mother and father.

His mother and father?

No, the parents of his wife. He hadn't even known whether they were still living, and there they were, still alive. Everything was exactly as it had been. The road from the station to their farm. Perhaps a little barer, but it might only have seemed so to him. It was autumn already, with the harvest in and the fields turned over, many crows. On the right there had been a reddish-blue field of cabbage stretching far into the distance—and you could smell it, too. But on the left the meadows rolling toward the hollow were cropped very close. And their road had been slippery and the ruts full of puddles, exactly as before. A heavy soil, very heavy, it stuck to one's boots so one had to be careful to keep from slipping. And the whole time church bells ringing in the countryside. Only when he had reached the point at which their house is first visible had they stopped.

The Prosecution interrupted with: All right, this landscape wasn't really important! His wife had been living with her parents?

No, no.

Well, where?

He hadn't known until he saw her parents. He hadn't known for sure whether she was still alive.

Tell us where she was living, if you please.

On the other side.

The other side of what?

Oh, in the house on the hill on the other side of the brook.

Good, so she was living in this other house?

Yes, strange, isn't it?

The defendant seemed totally absorbed in his memories. It was obvious that he had forgotten that he stood before a judge. He started when the Prosecutor addressed him again.

"We are interested only in how you came to marry your wife. You will omit everything else," he warned.

"What would you like to know?" the defendant asked.

"Just precisely what I just asked. Are you making fun of me?" The Prosecutor was losing his patience. "What is the meaning, for instance, of the remark that your wife saved your life?"

"Who made that remark?"

"You did!" said the Prosecutor in triumph. "And in case you don't believe me, I can show it to you in writing. It's in one of those letters of yours which your wife kept. I admit the letter's a few years old. Would you like to see it?"

"No, thank you. I will take your word for it."

"Well? What is the meaning of this utterance?"

"People shouldn't read old letters . . ."

"You've said that already. Privately, you can think what you like, but you must admit that the interpretation of old documents becomes a court's business, if it expects to throw light on certain difficulties."

"None of that has anything whatever to do with this Court."

"Please leave that decision to us. Just answer me clearly, in a few words, what you meant by this remark to your wife."

"I would have expressed it differently—now."

"Does that mean that today you no longer believe that your wife saved your life?"

"Then it was certainly correct if I wrote her in those words. There must have been a reason for it."

"And you are unable to recollect this reason?"

"Yes."

"Or, do you *prefer not to?*"

"We are not going to get any further this way," the defendant told the Judge. "An expression like that is a blade of grass a man pulls from the roadside and sticks between his teeth. Or something to eat offered a hungry man. Who can remember anything precise about it a few minutes later?"

The Judge asked the Prosecution if it wouldn't be better to drop this point, but the Prosecutor insisted on it. He was of the opinion that here they were confronted by a conscious attempt on the part of the defendant to cover up.

Cover up? The defendant picked up the phrase. Yes, it struck home . . . Everything was a cover-up, but hardly conscious. Nor was a court likely to lift this particular veil . . . They should bear in mind that he, the defendant, had traveled the whole night through and was a little shaky and fatigued. Most of all, on the road to her parents' house. "If I had asked for information to begin with, perhaps I wouldn't have gone there. But the only man to be seen on the platform was the stationmaster, and he was talking to an engineer next to the baggage car. And on the ramp of the freight shed sat three young farmhands, as one sees them on Sundays in small stations like this, waiting for girls who are in church. They were so young they couldn't have known anything; that's why I didn't ask them to begin with. And I met no one on the road. Everyone was in church. And her parents' barnyard, too, lay deserted among the fruit trees. Not a soul to be seen. No dog barked. Not a wisp of blue smoke from the chimney. It was Sunday morning. And I had traveled all night."

"Be that as it may . . ."

"No, there is no 'be that as it may' here, Mr. Attorney! You must realize that I had never expected to see any of this ever again. For many years I had firmly believed that they were all dead, her parents,

and my wife too, and if I dare mention this without
receiving a reprimand from the Court, I had long
considered myself dead as well. I beg the Court's
pardon: this must sound very strange, when for me it
was only too normal. I was living in a big red building with innumerable dark corridors and stairs and
doors. Doors, and more doors! No one ever cleaned
his small window, so the people behind each one
could save on curtains, and from attic to cellar it
smelled of cats, onions, and dust. There was never a
moment's quiet in this building. It was a madhouse—
or hell. Women gossiping from kitchen to kitchen as
they hung the wash out the windows; the crying of
children and the scolding of mothers; running in the
corridors and stairs, doors slamming and carpets
being beaten into rags and the jingle of keys; and
pots knocking against dishpans during washing-up
hour; the whistling and banging of the water pipes—
sometimes they banged so, the pipes almost burst—
and the rush of water in the toilets. And when the
men came home from work or when they got up to
leave again before day even began, there was such
stamping and a noise of gargling and confused conversation and often shrieks and the sound of something heavy knocked down, then the groaning of the
beds, and that snoring, day and night, without letup;
no quiet. And faces beyond counting! One knew
them all from having seen them; but not really, one
mixed them all up. And in summer, such swarms of

flies! It was like an oven. The red walls soaked up heat and never let it out. That's where I lived."

"What sort of building was it?" asked the Prosecutor.

"I believe you would call it a slum. The name fits the thing. The people who live in these buildings are insurable. Yes, all this is insurable."

Since there was laughter in the courtroom, as at every other mention of insurance by the defendant, he considered it necessary to turn once more to the public and add for emphasis: "It can be insured till the end of time. That's our business."

The Judge rapped on the table with his pencil. The Prosecutor continued: "Good, so you lived in this— slum. But what brought about your departure—your traveling all night, as you've told us—to look for your wife?"

"Chance."

"Please describe this 'chance' for us. Be as brief as possible."

"I had believed it was impossible to leave this building. I had never kidded myself that I'd come to terms with it. All I did was sketch something in the grime on a windowpane and that was it. Immediately I went to the rental office and asked the girl who always sat there. The office was very small, just room for a typewriter and a filing cabinet—all the available space was given over to rentals. For that reason it smelled very strongly of the girl . . . She told me I could simply leave the building by the side door—that wasn't so noticeable. I'd never have thought of it myself. And then I did leave the building by the side door and went straight to the station. That is all."

"You were not yet an insurance agent?"

"No, the idea only came to me later. I was working in the office of an accountant then. I worked an adding machine. My salary wasn't much."

"Good, let's get back to your wife. How was it when you first met again?"

"I walked very quietly to the house where her parents lived—quietly because everything else was so quiet. I didn't want to frighten anyone. I opened the front door—a front door is never locked in the country. But there was no one. The front hall looked exactly as it used to, even the cupboards were in the same places. It was a rather long hall stretching right to the back of the house. Only the ceiling had been freshly whitewashed, of course—a vaulted ceiling, as I remember. And since everything looked so dead, I went back outside and pulled at the bell. The very same bell as in the old days. A small clear bell attached to a wire. If you pulled hard, it took some time for it to quiet down. It sounded jolly. I had always enjoyed pulling it before. But that hadn't often been necessary, because most of the time the door had been open. Or I used to walk around the house to the kitchen garden. Or right on back into the summerhouse. And this time, too, I was very careful how I pulled the bell."

"Let's drop the bell, it's of no interest to the Court. What happened after you rang?"

"I had to wait. I didn't have to ring a second time, though. Once was enough. Then I heard a chair pushed back in the living room to the left, not very loud, no; and for that reason I waited a little longer. But, except for the scraping sound made by this chair, there wasn't a sound. And there was no smell in the hall, it was that clean. Yes, it was Sunday morning—have I mentioned that? I can see that you are growing restive, gentlemen. I can understand that very well, and am prepared to give up this narrative. I don't tell all this willingly, and if I tell it at all, it has to be as I would tell it; for it seems to me that this quiet and the cleanliness of that hall are of great importance. As important as it was for me then after that long journey. My story will not bear impatience; nor was I impatient myself then, though I was hungry. That I heard no footsteps followed naturally from the fact that her father was in his stocking feet. Thick, soft socks; her mother knitted them from long-haired rabbits' wool. Her father looked somewhat smaller than I remembered, but the truth of the matter was, I'd never thought once about him. Nor had he ever been very large. He recognized me immediately and showed no surprise at my arrival, or survival. It was almost as though it had been my habit to pay them a call every Sunday morning, and I too showed no surprise. I was far too tired. He invited me into the living room and called into the bedroom: 'Mother, come here!' And the living room was as it had always been, not a piece of furniture had changed position. And then her mother walked out of the bedroom and I hugged her, something I'd never done before. But it seemed natural to her as well. But how pale she was! Heart or anemia, frighteningly pale. I didn't ask her anything, nor had she any questions for me. All I told them was I'd traveled the whole night through. Then her mother brought me a big glass of milk and placed a loaf of bread on the table, and honey too, brownish-yellow, a very fluid honey. And as I ate, her mother cried. Somewhere or other, their small radio was on, very low, a service very probably, since someone spoke for a long time and then there was a chorale. But all very low; it didn't disturb us. I had had to sit on the old horsehair sofa. In the old days, only the older people sat there in the afternoon over coffee and cake, while we younger ones sat on chairs. Even the spinet was still there. It had always been badly out of tune. And between several antlers hung the cuckoo clock, but it didn't work, the pendulum was still. We talked about my journey and the cabbage field and things like that. They didn't ask about my past at all. They had given me up for dead long ago and did not wish to hurt my feelings. Nor did I ask them about their daughter, for the same reason. Yes, they were very cautious. We had all made a mistake long, long before, that's why. No one wished to cast the first stone . . . And that's why her mother was crying; she was accusing herself, thinking: Now it's too late. I sat facing the windows, which I could look out through easily, though the ivy in pots on the windowsill grew right up into the eaves. I could see the slope on the other side of the brook. Cloud shadows hurried over the hill, and for seconds, sunlight. I didn't let those windows out of my sight—perhaps someone will come down that slope, I thought. But if I thought back to the old days, who could have possibly walked down that slope *but me?* The sun, too, was keeping to the brook at the bottom of the hill, as if too shy to light what was above. For the house was up above. This other house up there on the other side of the brook, gentle-men—I want you to appreciate the fact—had for-merly belonged to my parents. They had bought it and renovated it slightly so that we children would have a place to go in the summer. Every summer we spent several months there, and it almost seemed like home to us. No, not because the house belonged to our parents, but . . . but . . . Because the house in which I was then sitting had almost become home for me. The farming of the lands that went with our house, my parents had made over to the neighboring farm, which belonged to the parents of my wife. But the house had not been ours for some time, not since the death of my father, when it had been sold, I'm not certain just why—I was told we needed the money. I had never looked into the matter, having no interest in the past. I had no idea who was living there at the moment; I mean, it was no concern of mine. Often, as we sat there on the sofa and light and shadow changed places on the slope across from us, while we chatted and the radio chatted out our silences, even quieter, while her mother sobbed, it seemed to me this must be like after we've died, then come once again to see how everything used to be, with complete contentment, patient. Pardon me, gentlemen, for thinking such thoughts, but I didn't know then that my wife was living on the other side of that brook with her husband."

"You mean your wife had already been married once?" the Judge asked, astonished.

Yes . . . and no, the defendant answered.

How could that be? What did he mean by that?

According to the law that applies in this courtroom, his wife had been married, and blessed by the Church as well. But the law—he begged the Court's pardon, he meant no criticism of the law—erred in this case.

In other words, the marriage had never been consummated?

The defendant did not answer for such a long time that the Judge repeated his question.

The defendant shook his head. "I find it practically

incomprehensible that the law considers necessary the use of an expression which degrades mankind by uncovering our nakedness to such an extent that all one can feel is horror."

He had spoken softly, but before the Judge could reprimand him—which appeared to be the Judge's intention—the defendant continued in a louder voice: "That marriage could not be 'consummated' because my wife and I were meant for one another. We had violated this destiny, or held it violable. That was the mistake for which all of us were being punished, punished hideously; more hideously than any court of this world can punish. All the same, there were extenuating circumstances. Both my wife and I were too weak to take effective measures against our separation. And those who had separated us were caught up in custom. Her parents, on whose horsehair sofa I was sitting, out of rural and religious prejudices concerning their daughter's happiness, and those from whom I'm descended, from pride of class and money. All of them wished only for the best. And in this the destiny which we transgressed is more severe than this Court: there are no extenuating circumstances! The transgressor cannot escape the punishment mercilessly executed upon his person. I would like to call it a death sentence. And all this came to mind, too, as I sat there on that sofa."

"That will do," the Judge said. "We must cut all this to a bare mimimum." So all that, about his wife having married, living in the other house, he found out at this time, from her parents.

Not at all, it had been the sun . . . Suddenly the sun had dared climb a little higher and had shined upon the other house. It had reflected from one of the windows up there, perhaps because it stood half open, so strong that it had almost blinded him down in the half light of the parlor. Almost as though someone had playfully made a sign with a pocket mirror. And it even came from the window of the very room where as a child and as a young man he had always slept. And not simply slept, because long, long ago he had sat at a table before that window and looked across the slope and brook . . . And her parents, too, had noticed this light that darted across to light him up. Words were no longer necessary. He got up to go over and pick up his wife.

The marriage was annulled, or was there a divorce, the Judge wanted to know.

Such formalities had been put into the hands of lawyers, the defendant replied. "Why not, when we were all in agreement?"

"And how did the husband behave?" asked the Prosecutor.

"What husband?"

"Your wife's first husband."

"I'd known him for a long time. He had been born and brought up in this neighborhood. As children we had played together, and fought, too. Cops and robbers down by the brook—which we defended and into which we pushed one another. We had all been part of the same gang. Now, though, he was drinking. He was so unhappy, but refused to admit it. My wife told me all about it. She said I'd come in the nick of time. He was unaware of any transgression. He had bought house and property and attempted a marriage with a girl he had known since they'd been children, and couldn't understand why it wasn't working out. He was innocent. We had to help him; he needn't suffer any longer for our mistakes."

"And he agreed to this immediately?"

"Immediately?" The defendant shrugged his shoulders vehemently. "There's a happy end. You can't know in advance if it will work out . . . But he remarried very soon. My wife told me beforehand whom he would marry; she already knew well what he only found out later. She was the daughter of neighboring farmers. He acted as though she were nothing to him, but my wife said they were meant for one another. And now they have children, too."

"Are you or your wife still in touch with him?"

"We heard about him when my wife's parents were buried. He bought their house and property—of what use was it to us? And with the money my wife got for it, I set myself up in business. Her parents died soon after this meeting, her mother first and a few weeks later her father."

"So there isn't the least possibility that your wife

has returned to what we might still call her home?"

"If you only realized how absurd that question is, gentlemen! Perhaps you've allowed the sunlight beamed from her window to fool you into thinking all was happy there. It was only a reflection. I wouldn't let myself be taken in; the light which shone from that mirror into the old folks' parlor no longer had warmth: nor could it dry her mother's tears. So I walked slowly across fallow fields and brownish meadows and over the old bridge that had lost its railings. As children, we often sat there and splashed in the water. Over and over, a solitary crow got up and headed croaking for the nests in a grove of oaks. All the while, distant church bells were ringing—perhaps there was a funeral and that's why this Sunday morning they rang so much. The sound was sometimes near and insistent, only to be blown afar suddenly like the whispering of a distant ocean. Otherwise, there was silence. Even up on the hill, where I had to walk around the house to get to the entrance, all was silence. Their old hunchback servant was scouring a wooden tub. She must have been hard of hearing, or perhaps mute, because all she did was point over her shoulder into the house with one thumb. I walked in. Half-light filled the hall. The great tiled stove was lit, and some pieces of crockery were on the white, linden-wood tabletop. Yet the house hardly looked inhabited. I climbed the stairs—I knew it all so well—and gently opened the door to my old room. The blinds were down, creating twilight in the room, so the only light that came through between the slats patterned the floor. The room was white and bare, neither pictures nor flowers. My wife was sitting on the bed. She had been waiting for me. I told her that to reach her I'd traveled all night. I had closed the door behind me, gently, and remained standing there—I had to have something to lean against. She asked if I'd brought her anything. No, I don't own a thing, I explained. Then we were silent for a long time, until she said he was in an inn in the next village but would get up shortly and be home in half an hour. Yes, this very moment he has become restless, but he doesn't know why. He will drink the glass that stands before him and leave. He isn't drunk, he's never drunk, but he is always at a loss. You'll have to talk to him when he gets here. As soon as we hear him, it would be best if you went down to meet him. You realize you're going to have to have a drink with him . . . Is that anything to you? No, I told her, it's nothing to me. Then we fell silent again and listened for him. But it was still too early. He was on his way, but he walked very slowly. In the room, the church bells were inaudible—they might even have stopped ringing. He'll be mayor, you know, she said. Really! He's the most capable farmer in the neighborhood, and very well liked. He's successful at everything. But you came just in the nick of time . . . A little later, and he'd never be mayor. He mustn't be drawn into this mess of ours, it's not his affair, and he's absolutely blameless, you must remember that. Yes, I know, I said. They think I'm sick, she said, because that's the only way they can explain my condition and also because they realize that often I wish I were dead. Naturally, that frightens them, and I'm doing them a grave injustice, allowing them to see it. But sometimes I simply can't help it; I didn't know where you were and whether . . . I traveled the whole night through, I said quickly. Yes, and it's good you finally made up your mind, she said. Time, yes, there still is, but you came just in the nick of time. But you're going to have to have a drink with him; that will make it all easier. Your breath will smell a little, but what's the difference? Outside, it will dissipate quickly enough. Sometimes I hear him snore at night. Oh, I feel such pity for him! He could already be mayor, and he snores so pitifully. He sleeps over there on the other side of the landing, where your sister used to sleep. Your parents' room is still empty. The old servant sleeps over the stables. You realize they all think I'm sick. Doctors have visited me, and I've laughed in their faces. You won't find anything wrong, I told them, but they wouldn't believe me. I was even sent to the hospital once, which cost us money, for nothing; very embarrassing for me. I endured it all because they expected it of me and to show I meant well. My god, what didn't they plan for me! They tried everything in the book, all they had

learned in medical school. I gritted my teeth; I would
rather have been one of our calves. They live a better
life, even if in the end they are slaughtered. They're
not told that. They frolic about the meadows, burst-
ing with contentment. And the comical piglets! I
can't help laughing whenever I see them zigzag like
lightning across the barnyard. And there, on my windowsill this summer, three little green finches sent
their cries all over the valley, fluttering their tiny
wings until their parents came back and stuffed
something into their bills. Can you imagine how
those birds had to slave, hearing those cries from the
other side of the valley? But we can talk about that
some other time. I would ask you to sit on the bed
beside me, as you must be awfully tired if you traveled all night. But there's no sense in that now; he'll
soon be here. And besides, I can see you better if you
stay there by the door. Everything's so different.
Don't take it amiss. I know very well you would like
to be sitting here next to me. And it's your room. I
shook my head. Yes! Yes, indeed, it is, she said. Don't
try to kid *me*. You couldn't if you tried. Were you
over there with my parents? Yes, I said, I was and I
had a glass of milk. Some of their honey, too . . .
My god, she said. But here it's schnapps you'll have
to drink, with him. For custom's sake. It wouldn't be
proper for you to refuse. Sometimes the whole house
smells of it. I don't much like it, the smell disturbs
me, but this once there's nothing to be done about it.

You must think of him, not us. You'll just have to grit your teeth the way I did, then it's all right. For him, at any rate, it's not too late, you've come just in time. Do you think that for us, though, it may be too late? I asked very gently. Who knows, she answered. And it isn't important enough for us to think about now. Perhaps if we could banish the thought that we have suffered unjustly, we'd be granted a respite. You know what I mean, lust for revenge. But that is so very difficult. I am not sick at all; they never found a thing wrong, and they examined everything. Even in the hospital, they couldn't find anything wrong. But how could they? I am perfectly healthy, I'm like any other woman, believe me. For I would scarcely ask you to drink with him if I were sick. In that case I'd just cry, probably, and send you away again. Believe me, I could very well have been the mayor's wife. But in that case, Mother and Father should never have sent me to the Sisters for schooling. They meant well, they only wanted me to have a better education; it's all easy enough to understand, yet the source of so much misery. For never again would I be able to become the mayor's wife, no matter how I might try. Think of it, I never read another book, not one book more. They even suggested that. They said: Now try a book, you used to like to read. But no, I had the books removed without even looking at them, once I set my mind on doing all I could to become the mayor's wife. All the same, it didn't work. If the mayor were standing there in the door the way you stand there now . . . No, he never stood there like you—he hasn't traveled all night. But you know him very well, you used to play together as children. Yes, he stood there like a boy who had come running, very fast; perhaps to be the first, completely out of breath, all hot and red in the face from the exertion, and suddenly had to put on the brakes, so as not to collide with me. And each time it frightened me so, that nothing I could do helped, and they wanted to put bars in my window. Yes, one morning the blacksmith's apprentice was here; he'd put his ladder up outside and climbed to my window to take measurements. I spoke with him and told him bars weren't necessary, I wasn't going to run away. So they stopped. But terror was strangling me, and once I couldn't keep from vomiting. Don't be angry with me for telling you this. I cleaned up myself, because it's really too unpleasant a job to fend off on someone else. I've told you about it only because in the old days we used to tell each other everything, and also so you won't think I'm sick. All this has nothing to do with sickness or health, but try to explain that to *them*. You simply cannot explain it. Do you remember how we used to sit in the summerhouse over there? Or down by the brook? And how quietly we used to creep across the moss in the forest; not even a deer could hear our steps, nor could we ourselves, up among the bluebells and the blueberries. I never

went there again, though it's not far. I didn't want to
make things hard for myself, but I'm the same as I
always was. You can't believe that, can you? You're
wrong, I believe you, I told her. Really? Yes, I replied, otherwise I wouldn't have traveled all night to
get here. And what have they made of you? she
wanted to know. The same kind of things happened
to me, I said. My god, she said, I used to think so
often how you must wonder, poor thing, why you
weren't happy with some other woman. And there
really are so many beautiful women . . . Yes, that
explains why I took such pains to become the mayor's
wife: I knew that if I could, then you would be
happy, too. But, unfortunately, I got nowhere. And
you really haven't brought me a thing? No, I replied,
I have nothing at all. Oh, it's not important, she said.
Afterwards we can go over to my parents' for a moment, to say goodbye. I'll get them to give me money
for the journey. And you won't be ashamed to travel
with the likes of me? Why should I be ashamed? I
asked. I don't have any city clothes, she answered. I
don't even know what they're wearing this season.
We'll take care of all that, little by little. We'll have
to be guided in everything by what others do, so we
won't attract attention. Look, I really have nothing
against your sitting here beside me. It's not that, it's
just that it no longer makes sense. He's here now, and
you've got to go down and talk to him. So I left her
and went back downstairs. He wasn't drunk, but his

eyes were bloodshot and glassy. We took our places at the table with the white linden-wood top. He took two bumpers from a wall cupboard and poured schnapps from a demijohn. The whole room smelled of plum schnapps. We talked about mutual acquaintances from the old days. He told me what had become of each of them. We also discussed agriculture and the political situation and drank all the while. That is, we were *waiting*. And then my wife came down, dressed, to say that she'd thought it best she take a look in the kitchen, because it was almost midday and the servant ought to have cooked something really good for him. At that point he burst into tears—it wasn't the alcohol. He was a big, strong young fellow with a fresh, red face. It is terrible to see the tears stream down such a man's face, and he not able to do anything about it. But, truly, it was better for him this way—he had just stumbled into all this. Yes, and then we left."

The defendant paused for a moment and then continued: "I have told you what can be told. I cannot judge whether it will satisfy you. I was not at all willing to discuss this subject and only did so because the Prosecution considered it necessary to ask questions about it. And I did not want to give the impression that out of ill will I was trying to conceal something. It is possible of course that what I have said may be of help to the Prosecution, but it is equally possible that it will be led to totally false conclusions. I beg your pardon, Mr. Attorney, for allowing myself such an observation. I have been honored with the qualification 'dependable.' Now, you will understand that after this there was nothing else for me to be. I know that my life has been irreproachable, irreproachable to the point of tedium. People like my wife and myself don't dare allow themselves the pleasure of starring in their own little novel—just to make life less boring. Everything had to appear so 'irreproachable,' so smooth, that anyone who meddled with us out of curiosity would find his hold slipping, and since that's unpleasant, would leave us be. No one would have believed us if we had simply said: It would be better for you if you kept hands off. He would have believed it as little as this Court when admonished in the beginning—I actually implored you—to arrive immediately, without further ado, at a verdict of guilty. Unfortunately, no one listened to me." The defendant sighed. "But what I wanted to say: If my wife and I never for a moment fooled ourselves into believing that our irreproachable private life was anything more than window dressing for the outside world—all the same, it had its limits. Children, for instance, gentlemen. That seems to be a question of burning interest to you all. And I admit that for perfect camouflage children are a necessity. But we found it impossible to bring children into this world just to have proof positive, a sort of certificate of citizenship bearing the motto: WE AREN'T ROCKING

THE BOAT! Should I have gotten my wife with child?
Should I have ruined her by making a mother of her?
And what would have happened to those children?
In our case—no, please don't get excited—children
would have been an attempt to defraud the insurance
company. And it doesn't take a district attorney to
tell me that these words are subversive in the eyes of
society. I fancy I am better able to express your point
of view than you are yourselves. In any case, it is absolutely essential for me to leave the structure of
your laws untouched. But why do you provoke this
very danger by attempting to delve into something in
which your laws no longer obtain? No, I beg your
pardon, gentlemen, I am not pleading my own case;
it's only that I'm *concerned*. On the contrary, I want
to confess that I have never rejected the idea of a
court passing judgment on me. I have been looking
for just such a court. It would have been an immense
relief for me if I had been condemned; I would have
slept soundly again. But every time I believed I had
found such a court and walked confidently into the
chamber to put myself at the judge's mercy, I was
horribly humiliated and disappointed to see that the
bench was vacant, and that I myself had to take the
judge's part to decide my own case. Who is up to
that? What is expected of me? How could I possibly
be so mature as to concede 'extenuating circumstances' to myself? For extenuating circumstances
mean that others bear part of the blame, that one is

having one's revenge. Therefore, I have so far refused myself the death penalty. And, equally, I hesitate to condemn myself to the severest retribution which the Court can hand down: to exist everlastingly in the certitude that I have failed my possibilities. To continue as a failure. A lost soul who only produces lost things."

The defendant looked at the floor. One had the impression that he was meditating on what he had said. Expectant calm filled the courtroom. Then the defendant looked up with a smile and said: "Those are all words which have no place here. I beg your pardon, your Honor. Wouldn't it be a good idea if from now on we kept to those things which you call 'facts' and on which your laws are competent? Once more, I assure you that I am ready to help in every way. I will try to think as a court must think. As an insurance agent, I have had some practice in this. Above everything, I shall do all I can to avoid being carried away into utterances that only make sense outside. They only prolong this hearing painfully."

After a short silence, the Judge glanced at the Assessors, the Prosecutor, and the Counsel for the Defense. Then he said: "We thank you for your detailed account. We refrained from interrupting you, and I do not believe either of these gentlemen would wish to comment. The Court is particularly happy to hear that you will give it your assistance during this hearing. And to take immediate advantage of your offer, I would like to ask, as much outside the custom of the Court as your remarks were, and just this once, a very personal question that came to me as I listened to you. Wouldn't it be simpler for us all if you told us right off or told me if you prefer, where your wife is hiding?"

"But that is precisely the one question which I am unable to answer," the defendant cried. "If I could answer that, I certainly wouldn't be standing here. I suppose . . . I can imagine . . . And I am talking to you personally, your Honor . . . I can imagine that my wife is still alive. Whether still as my wife, or otherwise, I cannot say. Indeed, why shouldn't she be still alive? A perfectly healthy person . . . All the same, she has—how shall I put it? She has disappeared from my field of vision, and this has left me rather at a loss. My eyes may be at fault. Or perhaps . . . But these are only suppositions, your Honor. Perhaps she was afraid of freezing to death and shook loose of me and went on. Or . . . But a man hesitates to say this—it sounds so presumptuous—or left me because she believed she was standing in my way. But I am only saying this to you personally, your Honor, because you asked me personally. If you please, it was all off the record . . ."

The Judge's attempt to give the hearing a new direction or even bring it to a surprise ending had obviously misfired. Not without a sigh, he leafed through his papers.

"Very well," he said, "the taking of evidence continues." The Judge pleaded with all parties to avoid further digressions. He wanted to know what else had happened that evening. Would the defendant make as precise a report as possible. Even trivial details could be of the greatest consequence in certain situations.

Nothing special had happened, answered the defendant. They had eaten dinner at seven sharp, as always.

Would he try to recall their conversation at the table.

They never talked very much.

There had been no argument?

No, why should there be? They'd had fried fish.

Why had he mentioned that?

Only because he had been asked to include trivia. They ate fish once a week. His wife believed fish was good for one's health, that's why.

And he didn't agree?

Why? Why shouldn't fish be good for one's health? It was always obvious that fish was on the menus from the moment he opened the door, because of the stench when it's fried.

Could he have made some remark about this stench which his wife might have taken as a slight?

Not at all! His wife asked him if he liked fish. She always did, because, quite naturally, she did not wish to set before him anything he did not like. And he had assured her every time that he liked it very much. It had been the same that evening.

The defendant seemed to give considerable weight to these filets. It suggested that there was more than met the eye.

No, he did not give them any weight at all! In the end, it was a matter of complete indifference to him what he ate, what was set before him. At the most, he could say that fish was more unavoidably noticed. Because when the stench of burning grease greets one as one opens the door, the thought involuntarily crosses one's mind: *what, again?*

What, again, meaning?

What, another week gone by? And that gives one a start, naturally. One could even say that for an instant one feels nauseated. But that has nothing to do with the filets as such.

Perhaps his wife had noticed this nausea?

No, impossible; the instant had been too brief for that, and anyway, the nausea had been more mental than physical. And besides, if she had noticed it, she would certainly never have served him fried fish again.

Very well! Enough of this fried fish. And the rest of the evening?

The table had been cleared. His wife had shaken the tablecloth out the window and then carried everything out. That was the nightly ritual, and the maid washed the dishes.

Had his wife spent more time in the kitchen than usual?

No, why should she have? Everything was as always.

And what had he done in the meantime?

Nothing. Oh, he'd walked up and down and smoked a cigarette. After dinner they always had a cup of coffee and he'd probably been waiting for that. Coffee his wife always insisted on brewing herself.

Very well. And then his wife had come back into the room with the coffee and sat down across from him? Or how had it been?

Just like that. Just like always.

He made uncommonly frequent use of the phrase "always, as always" . . .

How else was he to express the fact that things were happening as they always did?

Hmmm! Perhaps either he or his wife had experienced this "as always" particularly strongly that evening?

He didn't see anything about this "as always" that one *could* "experience particularly strongly"; on the contrary, this "as always" had been their only real protection.

All right. He could continue his story.

He had no story. Then he had probably closed the window.

The window? The window had been open all this time?

Of course! To air the place out. The fried fish, re-member?

Of course! ("Silence in the Court!" shouted the Judge.) Very well, anything else?

He had asked his wife if she wanted to see a movie. So they had looked at the paper. Out in the suburbs where they lived, there was only one theater and it was fairly unsophisticated. The picture they were showing was childish. Neither one of them, though, felt like taking the train back into town.

Had he gone to the movies often with his wife?

No, not more than was normal. His wife sometimes went in the afternoon, either alone or with an ac-quaintance.

Did he and his wife have any interests in common which occupied their spare time?

If the weather permitted, they walked along the lake in the evening from time to time. If possible after dark. Because of the other people. In these resi-dential suburbs, people lived as they do in a small town. Everyone knew everyone else, his whole story. You had to say hello and answer their "How's every-thing?" It was a nuisance.

He wasn't of a very sociable nature?

He didn't know about that. Anyway, he enjoyed being alone and often, especially in recent months. But that may not have been his fault.

Whose then?

The situation's. Or so it had turned out. During the

first years of their marriage, his wife and he had tried to live their life as they saw other people doing. Everything was so much simpler when one did that. For that very reason, they would have tried it. But it hadn't worked. They had certainly invited enough people over and had been invited to other peoples' houses in return. Acquaintances of his wife's in the neighborhood, and business friends of his. But always after one or two invitations the relationship had lapsed, never for any particular reason. It was just that the relationship never really came to life. And actually his wife and he had gone to a great deal of trouble when guests were expected; they had spared nothing. Really, when he considered other peoples' relationships and what others offered their guests, people should have preferred coming to their house. All the same, it somehow hadn't worked. His wife and he had often asked themselves how this could be, but never found an answer. Finally, they had given up, to avoid this sort of disappointment. Or rather, finally, by not seeing other people, they had ceased putting themselves in a position to be disappointed. Be that as it may, other women or ladies had from time to time come to see his wife. Chance acquaintances. His wife might have started a conversation with one of them in a store. But whoever it was, she was always gone by the time he got home in the evening.

"Everything you have just told us is corroborated,

more or less, by the depositions of witnesses," said the Judge. "Two of the women who recently visited with your wife were traced. When they were asked if it had been their impression that your wife suffered from the life she was leading, they replied that they couldn't remember ever hearing her complain. For all that . . . Tell us, didn't you ever feel that your wife might have need of more companionship?"

Certainly, and he too felt that way—hadn't he just explained that? It always pained him to hear her singing in the next room, even when the song was gay. She's singing in a vacuum, he'd said to himself, and she doesn't realize how lonesome that sounds. "Believe me, your Honor, we tried everything we could think of to change this; nothing worked."

"All of our witnesses agreed," said the Judge, "that your life was unusually regular. Actually, this should be considered praiseworthy, but why is it that these declarations put such unmistakable emphasis on the word *unusually?*"

"The truth is monotonous, your Honor."

"How's that? Which truth?"

"Truth is so monotonous that people find accepting it as such unbearable. Thus the expression 'unusually.' "

"So you believe you have a monopoly on the truth?"

"Oh, no. Everyone knows it; only, they evade it by entertaining lies. That's easily pardoned."

"I cannot help thinking," remarked the Judge angrily, "that on this subject you have something to hide. Or at least that at every turn you become evasive."

"Oh, no, I certainly haven't been evasive! Not once did I even attempt to evade this monotony. Why, I've even admitted my insecurity to the Court. Who would do that willingly?"

"But, on the contrary, the impression you're making on us is of a man who knows precisely what he wants."

"That is the result rather of my knowing what is impossible for me. I have experienced my limitations. And the experience was painful."

"For all that . . ." The Judge kept returning to the same subject: "To some extent your life and your marriage can be viewed as exemplary, but every positive statement about you betrayed a certain hesitation; one might even say scruple. Let me try to make this clear to you in another way. When people were asked what they thought of you, they never answered (forgive my unceremonious language): 'Oh, he's a regular fellow!' but rather, with almost imperceptible reservation in their voice: 'There's nothing unfavorable to be said about him . . .' Almost as if it were a miracle that *so far* nothing had come to light. Have I made this difference clear?"

"They never really trusted me," the defendant said with a smile.

"Yes, precisely. But why didn't they?"

They supposed that behind the monotony some-thing else lurked, that's certain. A vice or something devious, something that one was expected to try to hide. Because, without such a purpose, they could not imagine a man accepting such monotony. And even after one had demonstrated one's reliability to people who had felt uncomfortable with one, a mute distrust remained. By the way, he had done every-thing in his power to dispel it. For example, every Monday morning he looked in the paper for the name of the winning football team, so he could enter into conversation with the others—business demands this. He had become so expert that finally he knew more about football than men who really loved it. And it had been the same with politics or daily events. "All you need," the defendant said smiling, "is a certain feeling for what they'll talk about today. There's nothing to it." But then again it was tiring always to dissemble so that no one would notice one was. For instance, the psychological moment must be chosen for banging on the table with one's fist to communi-cate anger at political indifference or at the inexpli-cable bumbling of a favorite player. Possibly he'd sometimes chosen the wrong moment, and people might have noticed.

"Noticed what? I don't see what it is they might have noticed."

"That my private life, or what in Court you have

chosen to call my private life, was only window dressing."

"Private life!" exclaimed the Judge, surprised. "You said something like that once before. A curious observation, let me tell you. I believe we would say just the opposite. If need be, we might feel that our position in public life camouflaged our true nature, our private life . . ."

The defendant nodded. "Yes, I am aware of this widespread error . . ."

"Once more I will overlook the impropriety of your observation, defendant. No, please allow me to continue. This is not a conversation we're having, you're before your judge. Now then. I'd like you to consider the following. Isn't it almost comical that you, and you alone, accuse all of us of holding a 'widespread error'?"

The defendant bowed his head and appeared to consider this question. Finally he said: "Yes, it was most improper. I would like to drop the subject."

"Why?"

"Because I'm likely to give more improper answers. The fault lies with the questions put to me here, and with my situation."

"What situation would that be?"

"As defendant."

"Aha! If I understand you correctly, you mean that you must refuse to answer to avoid incriminating yourself?"

"Incriminating myself?" asked the defendant. Perhaps this was misunderstood; the Judge took it for irony and called him to order.

"So, in so many words, you refuse to answer?"

"I do not refuse to answer. I only beg the Court in its own best interests to desist from questions that will only lead to misunderstandings, which in turn will be interpreted as improper answers on my part. Your Honor, if only you would believe me: you cannot *incriminate* a man who has traveled all night to reach his wife. At the most he can be blown away, he's so exhausted. Wouldn't it be better if we kept to subjects which are within this Court's competence?"

"Once more I implore you to let the Court decide what is and is not its concern . . . What do you mean by 'window dressing'?"

"Anything that one can insure. These things are covered by laws, and if one doesn't keep within them, one will be condemned."

"Why, or against what, do you consider such camouflage necessary?"

"To gain a respite."

"A respite? Must you speak in enigmas?"

"I mean, it's an attempt to protect oneself from premature annihilation, by remaining unnoticed. For everything that has already been annihilated is full of hatred and seeps like a gluey substance wherever a vacuum exists to crust over the emptiness. Perhaps my attempt was unsuccessful. That's why I'm here."

The Prosecution came to the Judge's assistance. "In other words, you made the same use of your wife as you did of everything else, as—and I use your own expression—'window dressing'?"

"No, on the contrary; with her I remained open—on every front."

"So one thing your wife could never count on was total security as regards your person!"

"Mr. Attorney, that sounds so specious!"

"Defendant, you're avoiding the issue!" shouted the Prosecutor. "As a matter of fact, you know how to defend yourself very cleverly. But you shouldn't underrate the Court's intelligence. Did you make use of the same tactics against your wife: refusing to answer, avoiding the issue?"

"Tactics were never necessary—nor would they have worked."

"And you are certain that your wife found all this just as natural as you are trying to make us believe it was?"

"Yes."

"The Court has its doubts."

"Yes, I am aware of that. Have you ever heard a woman crying in the next room, Mr. Attorney?"

"You have already asked this question once. —So your wife often cried in the next room?" the Prosecutor asked suddenly.

"I can only assume that you have not yet heard these tears. They probably slipped past your ears without your noticing."

"Possibly. And why did your wife cry in the next room?"

"Mr. Attorney, I have been speaking neither of my own wife nor of a specific 'next room.' Nor have I been speaking of tears which have a cause, nor are they cried out so that another will overhear them. I have been speaking of the tears shed for the provisional nature of everything, which no consoling hand and no assurances can make any less provisional. Of course a man can stick his fingers in his ears, that's common practice. Will that do?"

"Whether or not it will do *for me* is of no importance. But let me tell you," the Prosecutor shouted in rage, "you treated your wife like no creature of flesh and blood!"

The defendant turned and looked toward the Defense; obviously he expected intervention in his behalf. Nothing of the kind occurred, and the defendant appeared astonished, but then said: "Your Honor, I do not care how I am treated, it's all the same to me. But I strongly object to such dehumanizing language used of my wife!"

The whole Court was surprised by this objection and by the indignant tone the defendant had used. The Judge did not believe it had been the intention of the Prosecution to insult the defendant's wife. Nor could the Judge understand how this remark could hurt the defendant's feelings.

"Flesh and blood!" said the defendant. "We are not in a hospital."

Once more the Judge assured the defendant that he must have misunderstood the Prosecutor. "On with the hearing! According to the testimony of your mother . . ."

"My mother!" interrupted the defendant. He wanted to know what his mother had to do with this.

"Your mother was called as a witness. Does this surprise you?"

Yes, it did come as a surprise, a big surprise. What could his mother know about any of this?

Not much, and for that reason the Court had not demanded her presence. She had remarked, actually, that at her age she no longer felt up to the shock such a hearing would occasion. "Why are you laughing, defendant?"

"Did I laugh?"

"Yes, you seemed to."

"I'm not in a laughing mood . . ."

"Very well. In her home town—your birthplace, if I am not mistaken—your mother was questioned by the local examining magistrate. I have the minutes here, but I admit we were unable to make much use of them. But again something catches our attention. As your mother was told of these proceedings—with all due care, you may be certain—her immediate response was to exclaim: 'I saw this coming!' But when asked to give a reason for her suspicion—yes, quite literally she was asked if she considered her son capable of such a crime . . .

"What's the matter? Do you feel ill?"

"It's enough to make one's flesh crawl," whispered the defendant. He had turned very pale and seemed quite unsteady. It sounded as though he were gritting his teeth as people do when they are going to faint.

"I can understand that you would have wished your old mother to be spared this questioning," said the Judge. "But you must realize that we felt forced to call her, in a case as murky as this. Naturally, as a relative, your mother was cautioned that she was not obliged to answer.

"Would you like a glass of water?"

"No, thank you," said the defendant, almost in a whisper. "Excuse me." He seemed to have regained his composure.

"Curious," the Judge mused, "that the questioning of your mother should make your flesh crawl, yet you face the event about which she was questioned with a coolness that alienates the Court."

"What makes my flesh crawl is the questioning of precisely the person least likely to speak the truth, and the fact that the Court feels it has to resort to such testimony."

"Was there tension between your mother and you?"

"No. Very young, I found it necessary to resolve all such tensions. May I ask how my mother answered the examining magistrate?"

"She did not give a reason for her exclamation," said the Judge. "On the contrary, she said she had just blurted it out without thinking. She hadn't meant to say anything of the kind."

"Aha!" said the defendant.

"And what do you mean by that?"

Accusation and apparent retraction—the very tactic of the voices from beyond the Abyss. They always maintain the proof of their guiltlessness. And let them have it; they are incapable of bearing guilt."

"Your words indicate no very high regard for your mother," said the Judge.

The Defense asked for the floor. He said that he, too, had taken it upon himself—and, indeed, without being asked to by the defendant—to look into the mother's situation, in spite of its having no direct bearing on this hearing; yet because a few of the mother's remarks had become known, remarks that might well be open to misinterpretation by the Prosecution to his client's disadvantage. For instance, said the Defense, in spite of the care with which his client destroyed all letters of a personal nature, one had come to light in which his mother complained that no

one cared about her, that everyone had deserted her.
If you were simply to read this letter, it certainly
sounded prejudicial to her son. But the truth of the
matter was quite different. Not only had his mother
sufficient savings to get by on, she was a person of
some substance. She lived in a five-room apartment,
luxuriously furnished, and had help. In her home
town she led the life of a respected older woman: visits made and returned, friends in for coffee, charities,
bridge, and church on Sunday. Besides all this, she
almost always had poor relations visiting her: daugh-
ters-in-law, cousins, friends from school, and so on. It
was these poor relations who spread the fairy tale of a
poor old mother abandoned by the world! Yes, a fairy
tale; even the Prosecution should have no trouble being persuaded of this by a few figures.

The Defense next gave an analysis of the finances
of the defendant's mother. In spite of losses due to war
and inflation, she could still be considered well-to-do.
And her income had significantly increased when her
son—and at this point the counsel raised his voice—
upon reaching his majority, *voluntarily* gave up an
inheritance left him by a grandfather, *in favor of his
mother*. The deed could be looked over at will in Pro-
bate Court. Yes, voluntarily; and, it would be well to
add, at a time when his mother had no need of this
money, whereas her son lacked any other source of
income. And later, before her son could be said to
have had much of an income of his own, he had con-

sidered it his duty—and again, though his mother was not in need—to send her a certain sum each year, in the last few years a considerable sum.

The Defense read the figures from bank statements. And this, by the way, explained why his client lived a life that seemed quite modest in relation to his income, and certainly when compared with the life his mother led.

And furthermore, his client had hired a responsible accountant to prepare his mother's tax returns and manage her estate—why, he even paid the man's expenses out of his own pocket. And his mother accepted all this as normal, yet she never stopped lamenting that she was deserted by everyone. Once a year without fail, his client had paid her a two-day visit with his wife, but they always stayed in a hotel so his mother would not be inconvenienced. Add to this that on her birthday and at Christmas they always sent her a splendid basket of delicacies. "If I describe all these things at such length, and very likely against my client's will, it is only because it astounds me, and must also astound the Court, that an attempt should be made by the Prosecution to blacken my client's reputation by drawing upon the testimony of a spoiled old lady whose comfort obviously requires a certain amount of complaining and tears. As for my client, the reproach should be rather that he took these complaints, although quite common among the elderly, and meaningless, too seriously; that, out of an exaggerated sense of duty, he took money, which he and his wife needed, to give to his mother, who did not."

The Judge asked the defendant if he had anything to add.

The figures sounded correct, he answered with a smile.

"And why did you always limit your yearly visit to two days?" asked the Prosecutor.

"Self-protection."

"What did you have to fear from your own mother?"

"Annihilation."

"Would you be so good as to explain what you mean by that?"

"Annihilation requires no definition."

"And you were of the opinion that for two days you could bear this 'annihilation'?"

The defendant shrugged his shoulders. "Perhaps I was not speaking of *my own* annihilation, Mr. Attorney."

"Then you mean your wife's? Or your mother's? Answer, please!"

"Your Honor, I refuse to answer until it is demonstrated that the law contains a paragraph which makes a son's visiting his mother for only two days a year a punishable offense."

Disorder in the Court. The Judge tapped on the table with a pencil and severely censured the defendant for contempt of court. "I'm being purposely provoked to a show of pride!" shouted the defendant, only to be once again called to order.

The atmosphere in the courtroom had reached the flash point. Neither Prosecution nor Defense appeared to believe it a good idea to exacerbate the situation by asking for the floor. The Judge riffled ostentatiously through his papers. Then he pronounced, in his most dignified voice: "This hearing will proceed."

Now they had reached the event itself. The Court had concerned itself at disproportionate length with the probable preliminaries of this event, disproportionate insofar as very little which could explain what followed had come out. Now, it must be admitted—yet this in no way prejudiced the final decision of the Court—that these preliminaries sometimes seemed totally unrelated to what followed; for, in examining the defendant's antecedents, no one would get the impression that this life could ever be threatened by disruptions. Be that as it may, the hearing so far had not completely missed its aim, since it had been made abundantly clear to the Court just how great a threat—whatever its nature—did indeed exist, and to what extent the regularity and almost pedantic order in which the defendant and his wife lived were totally artificial, served as mere "window dressing," to quote a favorite expression of the defendant's; were only for show. However, in attempting to gain some idea of the defendant's antecedents, they had to a certain extent kept within the bounds of the comprehensible; it had been possible, by drawing a comparison between the behavior of the defendant and the behavior of the average man, to take a position in favor or against. Even his most unusual remarks could be explained as the result of the deviation of an individual from the norm, however we might regard it. What followed next, however, seemed so patently to transgress the bounds of the comprehensible that the State Prosecutor, prior to bringing suit, had been quite uneasy about the Court's competence in this case. Thus the defendant had not been alone in doubting the Court's competence—a fact which naturally did not carry any weight in this consideration. Even he, the Judge, had occupied himself with this very question of the Court's competence, and he agreed completely with the defendant that the dignity of the Court would be impaired only if it vainly, and so to speak falteringly, took up matters outside its jurisdiction.

For all that, there was a lack of logical clarity here which must be suitably emphasized. In order once and for all to dispose of all doubts as to the competence of this Court, two principal considerations must be mentioned, the very considerations which had persuaded the Prosecution to bring suit. First, no court in the world could afford to admit in advance that any possible occurrence had the right or the might to place itself outside its jurisdiction. That would amount to the court's degrading itself to the subaltern rank of an institution concerned only with the upholding of commonplace regulations; and, in so doing, the court would call in question that universal security which was desired by the majority and for which the court bore the decisive responsibility. Therefore, any mention here of the "incomprehensible" pointed only to occurrences of which this Court, never having given a decision one way or the other, lacked necessary experience. However, the Court should not shrink from gaining this experience, and at once, if need be by enlarging its jurisdiction to take in areas in which until now nothing had come up for decision, as by tacit agreement the public avoided them, thus permitting the lawmakers to consider them nonexistent. In other words, this Court must accept as its duty the extension of its coverage to include the insurance of the public against the "incomprehensible"—if, as it now appeared (if only "appeared") to be the case, this "incomprehensible" could endanger that order which all desired.

And now he had come to his second point, and it was far more decisive: the event with which they were concerned, an event judged provisionally to be incomprehensible, had left them with an all too comprehensible fact. Or, they might say, however paradoxical it sounded, with a *gap* only too easily grasped! Quite rightly, the Prosecution had emphasized this point. In question stood the disappear-

ance of a woman, without, as yet, an adequate explanation; and until evidence to the contrary was
produced, the Prosecution could not be blamed for
its suspicion that the defendant was unlawfully implicated in this disappearance. Even if it should
come out that the defendant had had nothing to do
with it, still this inexplicable disappearance of a human being was enough to call the Court to action.
In its role of protector of society and security, the
Court could not countenance this situation, whether
or not the disappearance caused anyone to prefer
charges. Disappearance itself should be declared il-
legal. Therefore, he, the Judge, petitioned all parties
concerned, for the remainder of this investigation, to
avoid renewed digression into the undefined, urging
that they concentrate forcefully upon the concrete
problem before the Court: *Why* had this disappearance occurred? *Where* had it led? How closely implicated was the defendant? Was it to be considered a
crime or an accident? And, in the latter case, why
should the exact circumstances of this accident have
been covered up? Or was this a case of suicide? And,
if so, was the defendant an accessory, having driven
his wife to it? And where was the body? And, last of
all, was this a case of a real disappearance or only a
mock disappearance? After each of these points had
been decided, other questions would follow. For example, whether such an event was likely to recur,

and thus whether this case would become a precedent, his decision serving in the future as law.

He was aware of the fact, the Judge continued, that in practice it was unusual, almost improper, for a judge to present his summary by way of a commentary before the deposition of evidence had ended, as it might be interpreted as an attempt to influence the outcome. Nevertheless, because of the unusual nature of this case, he had decided to depart from practice, in order, if possible, to give a sharper outline to the hearing. It was his own impression that this case was far graver than it would appear from the wording of the accusation.

Did anyone care to contest anything?

If not, then the Court had arrived at the examination of what the minutes of the examining magistrate, following the testimony of the defendant, referred to as the "departure into the uninsurable."

The Judge stopped for a moment. A breathless silence filled the courtroom.

Of course, this expression meant nothing in Court, and decidedly it was the Court's duty to reject it absolutely. Nor, by the way, did the defendant, who had taken it from his profession of insurance agent, insist upon it. Thus, if the Court and the defendant had made use of this expression earlier, it had only been for lack of a more fitting phrase. They must be fully aware that this phrase indicated an as yet un-

known quantity, something which led to a human being's disappearance. It was this Court's business to
investigate these two possibilities: Was this "uninsurable" a fiction, to cover up an event or a crime? Or
was this really a case of the defendant's having been
so astonished by the novelty of what befell him that
he had involuntarily fastened on to it for aid?

"Defendant, would you care to remark upon the
preceding?" asked the Judge, turning full upon him.

The defendant shook his head.

"Or would you perhaps be in a position now to formulate this 'uninsurable' more precisely?"

Another negative.

"Very well, we will continue with the deposition."

He would now like to present a resumé of the testimony given in the preliminary investigation, the
Judge said, but if any point should remain unclear,
please to interrupt him. According to his testimony,
the defendant had kept his wife company from eight
until around ten. The maid had testified that she had
gone upstairs as soon as she was through in the
kitchen, and sorted out socks, then done some darn-
ing before she went to bed. Her room, like the bedroom of the defendant and his wife, was on the second floor. By the way, the maid had noticed nothing
unusual; she overheard no arguments that night.
And, indeed, the defendant maintains that there had
been no cause for an argument. Upon further questioning, he made the same stereotyped reply: "What

did we have to argue about?" As for the maid, she had been very tired and, to quote her own testimony, "slept like a rock." In any case, whatever took place later on the stairs did not awaken her. The maid corroborated the contention of the defendant that he and his wife were always quiet: "They scarcely even once spoke with each other loud enough to be overheard." Thus far the testimony of this witness, who only woke up much later, as the police entered the house.

So now the question was: What took place in these two hours, from around eight to approximately ten, during which time the defendant and his wife sat downstairs in their living room? This period could only be reconstructed on the basis of the defendant's testimony. He claimed his wife was busy sewing, but whatever it was she was mending was not found; possibly she finished it and put it neatly away that very night. A needle found downstairs beside a chair indicated at least that there was some truth to the defendant's contention. The defendant also reported that his wife had fiddled with the radio, looking for some good music, but had quickly turned it off, as there wasn't a station on which someone wasn't talking. He had been reading the newspaper but put it aside. They had also set up a hand of patience together, as was their custom. This evening it hadn't gotten very far. Certainly they had chatted, but he could not remember what about. The reason was once again the usual one given by the defendant: Why should they have discussed anything important? Around ten, his wife had gotten up and gone up to bed.

"We have uncovered nothing," continued the Judge, "to refute the defendant's testimony. We even went to the trouble of checking the radio programs that night for those two hours. And we determined that most of those stations which the defendant's radio picks up indeed played no music. This trivial fact—who among us would be able to recall something like this?—not only speaks for the defendant's general credibility, which the Court is only too glad to admit; it also proves that the defendant, during those two hours, was wide awake and attentive, rather than even the least bit fatigued or absentminded, as we might suppose. Indeed, that was the impression he later made on our first witnesses—the night watchman, for instance, who only a few hours later came upon the defendant beside the lake and took him for intoxicated.

"Excuse me, Mr. Attorney?"

"I have a question," the Prosecutor said. "Defendant, during the earlier interrogation you stated that you had not had anything to drink that night, since there had been no reason to, you hadn't felt sick. Did you mean to imply that you consider alcohol, in whatever form, solely a medicine?"

"Yes, that's about it," answered the defendant.

"Neither sociability nor your own pleasure ever makes you take a drink?"

"Hardly ever."

"Do you have any particular reason for your abstinence?"

No special reason. It was just he'd always felt alcohol falsified him.

"Falsified? How so?"

Unreasonable expectation, and such . . . Emotions intensified to the point of bewilderment.

"Has this caused you many unpleasant experiences?"

"Yes."

"Thank you."

The Judge again took the floor. In his summing up, he further wanted to add that an examination of the hours from eight to ten had given neither an indication nor the slightest psychological reference point for an understanding of what followed. "So you still maintain, defendant, that around ten your wife put away her sewing, got up, said good night, and went upstairs?"

No, she had also given him a kiss and begged him not to stay up too much longer. He had gotten up too and accompanied her, first to the front door and then to the door from the kitchen into the back yard, to make sure the house was properly locked. She went upstairs while he checked the back door. She turned out the light in the stairwell from above. There was light enough in the front hall because the bedroom door was open at the top of the stairs. They didn't do this way for reasons of economy; too much electric light bothered them both. It actually hurt.

"So nothing about your wife's behavior seemed unusual?"

No, it was exactly as it had been all those years.

"New for the Court, though, that your wife asked you not to stay up too late."

No, nothing new about it; she always said that. Women always said things like that. It was the same as Hello and How are you?

"You don't believe that women mean anything when they say these things?"

Hardly; it was just a habit. At one time of course they really were concerned about their husbands' health.

"And you wouldn't consider the possibility that in this respect you proved to be, shall we say, a bit hard of hearing?"

"Hard of hearing?" The defendant was astonished.

"Or, let us say, rather insensitive. Please reconsider carefully what you have told us. Attempt to reconstruct the scene. What I mean is this. You had been married seven years, right? Between married people, invisible connections exist, vibrations, shall we say, which a third party might not perceive, or, if he did, couldn't evaluate; and yet they are of *decisive* importance for the couple's life together, so important that overlooking or impairing these connections can put a marriage into doubt. Of course the Court can hardly concern itself with this, but all the same there's no getting around it. I don't know if you understand this."

"Oh yes, very well," said the defendant. He had been very pleased by that word "vibrations." In fact, the Judge wanted to know, didn't he, if that request not to stay up too long hadn't perhaps meant "Come on up"?

"Yes, if you must put it that way."

And, to speak very plainly and in the language of the Court, wasn't he being asked whether he had neglected his wife?

"To be sure, that question is closely related to what we are discussing. But I intentionally avoided this more general formulation. What the Court is interested in now is what happened on that specific evening."

"What importance you give to this one small sentence of my wife's!" said the defendant. There was surprise in his voice.

"What other method remains but giving importance to statements apparently devoid of it?"

"Are you serious?" The defendant sounded more surprised still.

"We have no reason to joke!" The Judge sounded as surprised. "By the way, you can always refuse to answer," he added.

"But in the end it isn't my answer that's important!"

"Whose then?"

"My wife's," said the defendant. This surprised all who heard it. The defendant glanced through the rows of spectators as though he expected to find his wife there. "I was just considering what she might answer if she were to come up here to help me. Perhaps she would laugh in your face, perhaps she would blush, and probably I would say to her: You don't need to help me, and you don't need to answer; these questions have nothing to do with us."

Everyone was so thunderstruck, and less by the defendant's words than by his manner, that they let him talk on. "I would protect my wife from the insulting suspicion that she had felt neglected. Or from the imputation that a woman only considers her existence acknowledged in full, and pleasurably, when a man must avail himself of her body."

"All these turns of phrase betray an unhealthy aversion," the Prosecutor interjected.

"Aversion? Shouldn't this sympathy with the body be called rather *affection*? Affection for this flesh so touchingly beautiful which suffers endlessly from the feeling that it's only a shell, to the point that it's almost impossible to deny it the consolation it desires. In order to find for it a little sleep, as for a sobbing child. Even when we realize beforehand how dearly this sleep is bought, with anxiety and alienation? And even sleep . . . Mr. Attorney, have you ever observed a couple the morning after? The sense of being lost, which their shame tries to hide, one from the other, by exaggerated activity? Quick, to the bathroom and shave! Quick, to the kitchen and prepare breakfast! Quick, to the office, to the grocery! And you can call this aversion? I have always considered this kind of anxiety the noblest part of the sentiment we call love, and indeed, the only hope. But it isn't just me and what I think. Mr. Attorney, I challenge you," and the defendant pointed with a sweeping gesture toward the public, "to place any woman present here on the witness stand and ask her whether or not she becomes terribly insecure when she is forced to accede to the body's desire to offer itself up!"

The Judge called the defendant most energetically to order. It was forbidden to appeal to the spectators. And besides, the defendant was certainly mistaken; what he had just said could only be considered, by the overwhelming majority of mankind, as a perversion of the truth. "Seeing, as we do, in physical love no alienation, but a union, rather."

Of course he knew that, declared the defendant. He might be said to know it better than others, since it was precisely this fear that the happy end might not be reached which had guaranteed him a princely income as an insurance agent!

"Defendant," cried the Judge, enraged, "you are not here before us to entertain the Court with cynical witticisms!" The public, too, was warned to behave more seriously. "We are investigating the disappearance without a trace of a human being."

The Defense seemed to consider it necessary to emphasize the fact that his client was no cynic, that actually the term "religious" fitted him better. The Defense even brought up various beliefs of former times which had taken an attitude toward sex similar to his client's. It is unnecessary to reproduce this confused speech word for word.

Several times his client signaled angrily that he should stop.

"We shall let the subject rest," the Judge decided. It would only lead to misunderstandings, which in their turn led to fruitless irritability.

Well, he'd been asked about "vibrations," the defendant mused, smiling.

"Enough! Enough! Let us leave vibrations behind and stick to what can be expressed in words."

The defendant had stated that his wife, some time between ten and twelve, but closer to twelve than ten, had come downstairs again, and indeed, seemingly without having lain down in between; this was to be inferred from her being dressed then exactly as she had been earlier. This also agreed with the testimony of the maid; when the closets had been gone through, only one dress was missed, the one the defendant's wife had been wearing all day.

"It wasn't a dress," the defendant corrected. "It

was a gray suit with a sort of double-breasted jacket. It was very becoming."

Thank you, a suit then, though this didn't matter. The investigators had also ascertained that neither bed had been slept in that night, although they had been turned down, and nightgown and pajamas were laid out diagonally onto the pillows as usual. Otherwise, the beds could be considered untouched. Only an impression in the quilt at the foot of the left bed, his wife's naturally, would lead one to think that she had sat there for a long time. On the carpet immediately in front, a woman's handkerchief had been found, in a crumpled ball.

"She had been crying," said the defendant, who had listened carefully.

Indeed, a chemical examination had proved this.

"Chemical?"

According to an analysis by the police technician, besides traces of his wife's perfume, there was also the residue of tears. Probably the handkerchief had fallen from her lap without her noticing as she stood up. Whether we could infer from this that she stood up suddenly, perhaps frightened by something, would have to be considered too. It was certain that this handkerchief, then, was the last identifiable object which had been in the hands of the defendant's wife before she disappeared without a trace. This justified its place among the exhibits, where it could be examined by the Court.

The defendant wanted to know if he might examine it.

Yes, certainly.

The defendant walked to a table where the handkerchief was offered him. It was a delicate, grasscloth handkerchief. The defendant held it for some time on his palm as though he were weighing it. Every eye in the Court observed him anxiously.

"The scent has left it," he said gently, and slowly laid it down again. "Perhaps that's because of the chemical analysis," he whispered as he returned to the dock.

The Judge wanted to know if he recognized the handkerchief.

Yes, he had given his wife three of them for Christmas two years ago. They had been rather expensive, but the saleslady had assured him that they were very high quality.

Good. By the way, the maid had recognized the handkerchief as her mistress's property. Did he have any other observations to make?

No.

Then why had he said: "She had been crying"? Had he known that his wife had been sitting upstairs on the bed crying?

No doubt of it now.

"You haven't understood me," the Judge said. "I wanted to know whether on that night, while you were downstairs, you knew that upstairs your wife was crying?"

No, he hadn't known.

"But could you think of some reason now why on that night and at that hour your wife should have been crying?"

Perhaps there was no reason.

What did that mean?

Sometimes people cry for no reason, and that is the only time it's real.

Had his wife cried often?

No, hardly more than anyone else.

"And what would you have done if you had heard her crying?" the Prosecutor asked.

It wasn't easy to say. Possibly he'd have gone upstairs to try to console her. But perhaps not. If there was a reason for her tears, then of course he'd have gone up, because a reason can always be reasoned away. But if it were genuine crying, the best thing was to let it run its course undisturbed.

"Don't you consider your attitude—I don't want to say 'heartless'—let us say, dangerous, at least, in the condition your wife was obviously in?"

Certainly it was dangerous, very dangerous perhaps. Dangerous for both of them, perhaps even more so for the hearer than for the person he hears crying. It's the helplessness. Ineffectual waiting-it-out, head bowed, and hands grasping the edge of the table to keep them from doing the wrong thing; nothing but wait and hope the crying stops of itself—it was horrible!

So the defendant stuck to his statement that there was no reason for these tears, the Judge wanted to know.

No reason? Again, that wasn't how he'd put it. Because, as everyone knows, there is always a reason. The reason without a reason.

"What is the meaning of this paradox, defendant?" demanded the Judge. He was annoyed. "We are getting nowhere. And I won't try to conceal from you that we are all under the impression that at this point there are words which you are holding back."

No, words were holding him back. He had nothing to hide. He had spoken as clearly as he could and flattered himself that he had spoken more clearly than most men would have. And it had been possible for him to do so because for hours and hours he had been able to eavesdrop, as it were, without clamping his hands to his ears in horror. Yet, all the same, most of what he wanted to say remained inexpressible; and it was better he didn't try to express it, since words themselves are distractions.

The Judge sighed. "You make it very difficult for the Court to believe in your sincerity. For one thing, there is the ease with which you pull the rug out from under our feet each time we believe we've gotten hold of the smallest certainty—and you do it with a semblance of logic and justice. It is precisely the cleverness of your tactics which arouses our suspicion. Why are you doing this? You must realize how your behavior arouses our mistrust. No innocent man would find it necessary to make such a blatant effort to camouflage himself. Won't you make things easier for yourself and for us by accepting the fact that nothing is more important to this Court than establishing your innocence. For once, consider this Court your friend, intent on freeing you from an unjustified accusation."

"But it isn't myself we're concerned with, it's my wife!" objected the defendant with some heat.

"Yes, yes, you have told us that several times already.

"Yes, Mr. Attorney?"

Could the defendant be implying that he had vowed silence to protect his wife? Perhaps because he had felt it necessary to take some guilt of hers upon himself, out of love or a sense of chivalry—and what did it matter at the moment whether this "guilt" was of a legal nature or not?

"Some guilt of hers?" asked the defendant.

"Let's drop the word 'guilt,' as it leads only to misunderstandings. Instead let us say 'motive,' or even 'whim.'"

"The word you mean isn't guilt, it's *fate!*" cried the defendant.

"A grand word. I thank you for the correction."

The Judge and the Prosecutor exchanged looks, and the Prosecutor shrugged his shoulders.

From all indications, the Judge continued, it must be considered certain that the defendant's wife did not go to bed that night as she usually did, for the reason that she was aware of her husband's decision.

Decision? interrupted the defendant. As though anyone could *decide* something like this. It isn't within our power.

Very well, they would substitute "awareness of the likelihood that something would happen that night."

Awareness? objected the defendant stubbornly. Even that wasn't possible. And happen?

"You are making unusual demands on the patience of this Court," the Judge interrupted. "I beg you to answer the following question without splitting hairs. How could your wife have been aware of your plans or suspect that a crisis was in the offing?"

The defendant did not answer immediately; but not, apparently, because he was looking for words; he feared, rather, that once again he would arouse the indignation of the Court.

They had been married seven years, he finally answered, and had lived less diverted by this and that than most people do, without children, without a social life. Thus they understood each other very well; neither was able to keep anything from the other; however unimportant the feeling, it was hardly secret; the other felt it immediately and felt a change then in himself. Often, one realized something about the other which the other could not even whisper to himself yet; one's secret thoughts, the possibility of change becoming open, real, yes, even dangerous only through the other. Of course, one could misconstrue the other's behavior, out of fear, but the mistake quickly corrected itself when one lived in the same house, breathed the same air, sat across from the other at the table, and slept in twin beds, even though . . . Yes, it was in sleep that one was often frighteningly far from the other, to the point of total invisibility, in spite of the very real proximity—and with no defense against this. Yes, it had been a little like what happened while people slept. He wished to beg the Court's pardon; granted that it could all have happened so differently, precision was impossible. The events of that night might have occurred the previous evening or might have waited another year, and under certain conditions might never have happened—that was what disturbed him most. This crisis, as the Judge called it . . . Yes, the question was perhaps whether his wife hadn't simply decided to provoke one because waiting had become unbearable when that "something" waited for could come to pass at any moment, but then again, might never come to pass, however long they lived. That must have been a terrible decision for his wife, so terrible, that he, the defendant, trembled to think of it, and felt guilty for not having been able to relieve her of the responsibility of making it. "Yes, it's even likely that I stand here for no other reason." But then again, as he had said, this might not be correct. Above all, the word "decision" was misleading; it seemed to him more like giving in, being swept away.

"In other words, you and your wife never discussed this?"

No, no one can.

"But now you yourself believe that your wife had considered this a possibility for a long time?"

Yes, of course. From the very beginning.

"Once again: Do you believe that the reason your wife did not go to bed as usual that night might be that she considered your departure into the "uninsurable" imminent?"

The defendant laughed. When asked why, he blamed this comical turn of phrase.

"That is not our fault," corrected the Judge. "If you would oblige us with a more fitting designation, we would gladly stop making ourselves laughable!"

The defendant begged his pardon. It had been the word "departure" which made him laugh. As though one "departed" into *that region* as one does for a short walk or even to go around the world. Suddenly one was *in it;* or, rather, one realized suddenly that one was in it; and, what's more, that he had been all along, that this "uninsurable" was everywhere one stayed or tried to stay, here in this courtroom as much as in an escape-proof cell, or out in the open; it didn't matter, and all there was left to be surprised about was how long one had tried to deny it.

"Let us leave this for a moment," said the Judge. "Let us go back an hour or two in that fateful night and look into what you were doing. After your wife had gone upstairs to bed, as usual—let us suppose this for the moment—and after you had closed the door to the living room, what did you do? Can you tell us a little about that?"

Why not? He had sat down at the table.

Very good. Why had he sat down?

What did that mean? Why, sat down to be seated!

"Enough of this laughter!" shouted the Judge to the public.

And what had he done after seating himself at the table?

Nothing.

Did he mean to say that he sat there approximately two hours *without doing anything?*

He might have smoked.

Did he smoke a great deal?

No, not really. Maybe three or four cigarettes. Sometimes, too, he forgot to smoke.

But no butts had been found in the ashtray. How did he account for that?

He had emptied the ashtray.

Really? Most peculiar. Why had he done that?

No, there was nothing peculiar about it. It had always been his habit to empty the ashtray into the trash can in the kitchen before going up to bed. His wife had asked him to do this years ago. So there would not be a stale smell in the living room. Admittedly, this would never have occurred to him on his own.

Very good. Accordingly, he had gone to the kitchen that night with a full ashtray and emptied it?

Of course, and why wouldn't he have emptied it that night like any other? And it was then, while he was in the kitchen, that things started happening.

"Just a minute! We will come back to that. Let's remain a minute longer with you in the living room. Did anyone visit you that night?"

"Visit me?"

"Yes, why not?"

"I *never* have visitors. Who would visit me?"

"But perhaps just *that* night . . . The room in which, according to your own testimony, you were sitting is on the ground floor. Thus, it would have been possible for you to let someone in without difficulty, without having to unlock either the front or the back door, and without anyone in the house noticing a thing."

"Why would I want to ask anyone in through the window?"

"The Court has to consider every possibility. However, footprints were not found in the garden, nor fingerprints on the window. The only suspicious fingerprints were found in the bathroom and turned out to be the plumber's who had repaired a faucet that afternoon."

"All this sounds like something from the annals of crime." The defendant had disbelief in his voice.

"It's about time you realized that until this Court dismisses the charge against you, you are indeed involved in a criminal case," said the Judge. "So you had no visitors. Were you called to the phone?"

"No, that wouldn't have been possible."

"Why not? You'd paid your phone bill, had you not?"

"My wife always takes the phone upstairs when she goes to bed."

"You did not mention this to us before."

"I didn't think of it. In any case, we've been doing it since we had an outlet in the bedroom."

"Very well. But why did your wife always take the phone with her?"

"So that I wouldn't be disturbed. I don't like telephones. Every time one rings, there's a moment of fright. But we need it in the bedroom at night because from time to time an anxious client phones to have something insured. Naturally, the insurance company has empowered me to take care of such cases. But this happens very seldom."

"And if anyone calls while you're downstairs, your wife always calls you to the phone?"

"Yes, of course. She calls down from upstairs. But, as I said, she doesn't often have to do it."

"Then your wife doesn't take the message and only give it to you later?"

"No. The clients feel more reassured if they speak to me personally. In business, things like that have to be taken into consideration."

"Hmmm . . . That's understandable. Tell us, can you hear the phone downstairs when it's upstairs?"

"No, not if the doors are closed. Only my wife can hear it then, strangely enough."

"Your wife? I thought you just said she had gone up herself?"

"I mean when by accident we've left the phone upstairs. Suddenly she'll say: 'The telephone!' and run upstairs. Every time it happens, I'm surprised. She must have much better hearing than I."

"So your wife gets many phone calls?"

"Not at all. Who is there to phone her? From time to time, of course, and if it happens during the day, she tells me all about it when I get home. At the table we tell each other everything we've noticed during the day. It's never very much—what ever happens to us? That explains why we tell each other the most trivial observations, things other people would forget immediately. We have no secrets from each other. Sometimes it was difficult to tell anything, because nothing at all happened. For that reason we kept our eyes open wherever we were: everything we saw, from people on the train to a dog in the street, was something to tell the other."

"You don't happen to know if anyone phoned your wife that evening?"

"That evening?"

"Yes, while you were sitting downstairs."

"But she would have told me!"

"Perhaps your wife forgot to. Or there was no time for it later."

"But she would have called down to me."

"Perhaps she had some reason not to."

"Well, what reason?"

"The call wouldn't absolutely have had to be for you . . ."

"Not for me? So someone did call her! Tell me!"

"We are asking the questions here."

"Who could have called her? In the middle of the night?"

"It wasn't that late."

"No, it's impossible."

"Why do you consider it impossible? You yourself just told us that usually you don't hear the phone ring when you are downstairs. By the way, it might not have rung. There is the possibility that your wife might have made a call."

"My wife might have . . . But to whom? You know something!"

"The Court is asking the questions here, not you."

"Oh, no! I mean, your Honor, in this case you must make an exception. Must we stick to stupid rules and regulations? The gravity of the situation demands more than that. The existence of *my* wife is at stake. And if you know anything definite, you have no right to keep it from me. I am her nearest relation, am I not? As far as you or this Court is concerned, this is routine, or some sort of game; or all theoretical, whereas I . . . No, it simply isn't conceivable!" The gestures of the defendant seemed intended to chase something away . . .

"Please, calm yourself, calm yourself," said the Judge. "And, by the way, I cannot comprehend your becoming so excited over the simple possibility of someone calling your wife."

"But just think," shouted the defendant hoarsely, "what that means, being *called*, out of the blue like that in the middle of the night, and worst of all, by telephone . . . Yes, that's it, the telephone! Suddenly it rings and then . . . No, it's impossible, it shouldn't be possible! Not by phone! What is a telephone? a cord, a little electricity, a membrane! It's terrifying, really. Because it would mean that we are all even more defenseless than I had supposed. No? And you believe someone phoned my wife?"

"Again I must ask you to be calm," admonished the Judge. "It is our duty to take into consideration every possibility, and among them there is the telephone."

"No, not by phone. I won't even admit the hypothesis."

"Very well, let's drop the subject. Tell us, do you know someone named Gruditz?"

"Gruditz? What has Gruditz . . . He has . . . He's a contractor. And a good client. What's wrong with Gruditz?"

"On a note pad next to the telephone on the table beside your wife's bed, we found the following: *Gruditz / Coverage*, dated that night"

"Then perhaps Gruditz phoned. Why wasn't he asked?"

"Mr. Gruditz will be called as a witness later."

"Gruditz a witness? Then why not now? That would explain everything."

"I cannot turn the rules and regulations on their head just to please you. Be that as it may, if it will calm you—according to Mr. Gruditz's testimony during the preliminary investigation, he actually did call, at quarter to eleven."

"So? What did he say? He must have said something decisive. But how could he have? My wife had never even met him!"

"If you would listen to me instead of exciting yourself unnecessarily . . . Mr. Gruditz phoned from a café in town. It had suddenly occurred to him that he hadn't taken out insurance on the new car that had been delivered that afternoon. He was afraid all of a sudden and therefore, though it was late . . ."

"Oh, and was this taken care of? Funny that my wife didn't say a word . . ."

"Once more I believe I have good news for you. To make doubly sure, Gruditz and Company telephoned your office the next morning and your secretary took care of the policy. The new car had not been damaged during the night . . ."

"I've been very lucky!" cried the defendant, visibly relieved. "Usually it's just at times like these that something does happen."

"Funny," the Judge remarked, "that the mere settling of this piece of business, and a fairly routine one at that, should give you such pleasure . . ."

"See here . . ." But then the defendant laughed. "Yes, forgive me, it really is rather funny. That is a habit of mine dating back to the days when I was still 'dependable.' Gruditz! What's Gruditz to us? He's a fine fellow, a typical contractor, but in the end, what does he *want?* And yet, it is good that things cancel each other out like that. Now do you see how much time you wasted with this business of the telephone?"

"Perhaps you would be so kind as to return the direction of this hearing to me," said the Judge. "And the matter is not so simple as you would like to believe. If Mr. Gruditz could speak with your wife without, apparently, your hearing anything, or her telling you anything, it is equally possible that she spoke to other people without your knowledge. Please do not interrupt me. Such calls remain a possibility at least, though the Court has no proof of them. Gruditz's call is of the greatest importance because it gives us a point in time. At a quarter to eleven there was still someone there who reacted to the telephone's ringing; and what's more, a woman. I say *a* woman because Mr. Gruditz had never met your wife and thus doesn't know her voice, and therefore we cannot ignore the possibility of some other person of the female sex having answered."

"How did she sound?"

"Defendant, you need speak only when spoken to. Assuming that it was the defendant's wife who answered the phone—the police investigation gives us no cause to support anything else—then Mr. Gruditz was the last person to have talked with her, if only over the phone. Now what I want to ask you, defendant, and please listen carefully, is: How do you explain your wife's not calling you to the phone—as she had always done—this time, when Mr. Gruditz made a point of asking to talk to you?"

"I . . . I don't understand it either. Perhaps . . ."

"Well?"

"Perhaps she was crying by then and didn't want me to see."

"Good, that sounds plausible. Your wife is said to have answered: 'I'm sorry, but my husband cannot be reached at the moment,' or 'I'm sorry, but my husband isn't here.' Mr. Gruditz doesn't recall her exact words. He thought it might even have been 'My husband is no longer reachable, I'm sorry.' "

"No, Mr. Gruditz must have misunderstood. I was

there all the time, downstairs; and my wife knew it. If only I could hear her voice, I'd know immediately . . . A voice is recognizable."

"If we accept the defendant's account, the question arises: What was taking place up there in the bedroom from ten to about a quarter of eleven? In other words, what was it during those forty-five minutes which caused the defendant's wife to alter her usual behavior? And what was it that caused her to cry—if this did not happen later? Any way we look at it, the possibility of another telephone call cannot be written off, a sort of last straw. If nothing more, Gruditz's call proves that the defendant need not have heard a previous or a later call. The maid, too, heard nothing; in any case, she was not awakened.

"Mr. Attorney?"

He had no intention of challenging the credibility of the defendant any more than his Honor had, but the Prosecution felt that a further possibility had not been taken into consideration. The defendant's wife could have come downstairs during this time.

The defendant claimed that he would have noticed that.

The Court could not be certain of this. Only a few minutes ago, when the telephone had been discussed, the defendant himself had stated that he was not as quick of hearing as his wife. And besides she might have come downstairs very quietly, in her stocking feet even. And perhaps she listened at the door to the living room and realized what was going on inside.

Going on inside? What could have been "going on inside"?

That was the very question they were concerned with! In any case, she might have heard something that made her cry.

Outraged, the defendant shouted that his wife didn't listen at doors. And in her stocking feet! It was grotesque. And even worse when there wasn't a thing to overhear.

Would it be possible that the defendant was in the habit of talking to himself?

Talking to himself? Out loud?

The Prosecutor saw no reason why not. It often happened when people were deeply involved in their own thoughts.

While one slept, perhaps, but then one wasn't in control; and *he* hadn't been asleep, he'd been *wide awake*.

Wide awake? The Prosecutor wanted to know why he had emphasized those words.

The defendant answered that these hours were always his most lucid. Perhaps his only really lucid ones. Actually, it had often been difficult for him to tear himself away. And if he did go to bed, it was only because he realized what he had to do the next day, and of course for his wife's sake, since she considered staying up late bad for one's health. Yet it always seemed to him almost betrayal.

Betrayal?

No, not betrayal, but something very much like it. The feeling one has if one fails to do something which one ought to do when the opportunity presents itself.

Had his wife known anything about this attitude of his?

His wife knew every thought he had, even when, as chance would have it, they were on different floors. Perhaps then even more clearly than when they were sitting next to each other.

The defendant ran out of words at this point. When asked by the Prosecutor why he did not continue, he said after a moment's hesitation that something had just occurred to him. A short time before this, they were sitting together one evening and his wife had said: "I pity you." Without apparent cause. They had been silent for a while and before that had only spoken of everyday matters; so it couldn't have referred to any one thing; and, too, it had sounded as though it came from so far away, from another room, a room in which the speaker was out of line of sight, or through a fall of snow . . . It sounded a little patronizing, although that might only be his imagination. In any case, he had immediately realized the danger in these words.

And? The Prosecution would like to know what he'd done about it.

Nothing. Like cotton wool, he had soaked up these words without resistance, so they wouldn't echo.

And what was dangerous about them?

The seduction of pity.

Seduction?

It so easily diverted one from the facts.

"That's over my head," said the Prosecutor. "But tell us, why did you describe this little scene?"

"It occurred to me only since the Court takes for granted that I had a visitor and my wife eavesdrops. Those are figments of the imagination, ungrounded in reality."

With his Honor's permission, he would like to return to that ashtray, the Prosecutor said. There was certainly no argument as to its reality. It had been found emptied but with traces of ashes, cigarette ashes at that. Unfortunately, the maid had already emptied the trash into the municipal ash can at the curb before an examination could be made. Otherwise they might be in a position to know how many cigarettes were smoked that evening, or during those hours.

Two or three, four at the most; hadn't he already said that? interrupted the defendant.

There was no proof, though. When had the defendant emptied that ashtray in the kitchen? Before his decision—or whatever they were to call it—or on the basis of this decision?

But he'd just emptied it that night like any other. No "decision" had been necessary. And earlier it wouldn't have made sense, because he might have felt like another cigarette.

"In other words, it was your intention to go up to bed, and therefore you took the ashtray into the kitchen?"

Yes, as always. Not a single movement different from the usual. Each had been worked out long before. "First I had to put the ashtray down by the sink so I would have both hands free for the lid of the trash can. Once, right at the beginning, the lid fell from my hand and the noise woke my wife up; she thought someone had broken into the house. Yes, and the moment I had the lid in my hands, that night I mean, I thought I heard something upstairs. The knob of the door to the bedroom does rattle a little. I was scared to death. It just can't be described."

"Why was that?"

"One thinks everything is the same, and one thinks that one's alone, then suddenly . . ."

"And you were still holding the lid of the trash can in your hand?"

"Yes, I suppose so. I was listening."

"You felt you had been caught in the act?"

"Yes, that's about it."

"And what did you do with the lid?"

"How should I know?"

"All the same, you emptied the ashtray?"

"Yes, I suppose so. Who can keep track of such things when he's frightened? And there was no longer any need to be quiet, as my wife was coming down the stairs."

"If it is agreeable, Mr. Attorney," said the Judge, "I would like you to put these later events aside for the time being. It seems more proper to me that we proceed chronologically."

He, too, was much more interested in what the defendant had been doing in the living room for two hours—much more than in that ashtray, the Prosecutor replied. "You claim, then, that you spent the whole time seated at the table not doing a thing?" he asked the defendant.

Possibly he had stood up once and walked up and down the room when his restlessness had been too much for him. But never for long.

What restlessness?

The restlessness of waiting.

Waiting? Waiting for what?

For nothing in particular. Just waiting.

Why hadn't he chosen a more comfortable chair then, the easy chair?

In an easy chair one felt imprisoned, unable to jump up quickly enough.

"Ah! You had to reckon with jumping up quickly, did you?"

"I have always lived that way," said the defendant. "And that's why it's better to sit at a table." .

"How odd," mused the Prosecutor.

"A person can push himself away from a table, or he can grasp the edge if he loses control."

"Did you think this was something you had to be afraid of?"

"No man living can know exactly how much he can bear. To claim anything else is mere boasting."

"And if I may ask another question: Have you often lost control of yourself?"

"Yes, it happens now and then."

"And how does it show?"

"There are no words to describe it."

"That night, too?"

"That night, too."

This last was spoken in such threatening tones that everything in the courtroom seemed to yield before it. One of the Assessors dropped his pencil; it rolled across the table and fell off. In the general hush, the noise this small object made in striking the floor seemed unbearable. The Assessor went red in the face and squinted in embarrassment at the Judge.

The Prosecutor leafed through his papers; he, too, seemed impressed by the defendant's answer. In any case, he gave up the line of questioning he had been pursuing. After an exchange of glances with the Judge, he began again by begging the defendant's pardon, as it were. However, this might have been nothing more than a ruse.

He asked the defendant not to take amiss his tiresome, indeed indiscreet inquiry as to what could have occupied him during those two hours. "And not simply *those* two hours, since you have told us that they were like so many others. Do you mean that night after night you sat at that table for two hours at a time without doing anything at all?"

"Some nights even longer than two hours."

"And this never bored you?"

"No, Mr. Attorney."

"I beg your pardon, but this is difficult to believe. You must have some hobby. Or it could be a vice. Did you collect stamps? Do you do crossword puzzles?"

A smile seemed to spread across the courtroom; the Prosecution had attained one of its ends: the tension had been lowered. "No, wait a minute, you must be a reader. Yes, all of us here have the impression that you are a well-read man. And that's excellent, none of us can read enough. In the evening, after the labors of the day, picking up a good book means something. Or did you possibly write poetry? Now there, that would explain a great deal. For we are told that writing requires great concentration, and also solitude."

The Defense took the floor. Was it compatible with the dignity of the Court that his client be made fun of?

"How could you even think, dear sir, that I was making fun of your client? I am only asking questions any normal man would ask and no one could take amiss. In my search for motives, it is possible that noble ones will come to light. Or could you have any doubts about the nobility of the motives that prompted our greatest poets to write their poems?"

"Really, Mr. Attorney!" warned the Judge.

The Prosecutor bowed to the Court. "But why don't you answer, defendant? Why do you shroud yourself in silence? Something must have happened during those two hours which has some bearing on what followed, or at least on what caused your wife's tears."

The defendant did not break his silence.

"Or do you keep a journal and find it embarrassing to admit it?"

"And where in the opinion of the Prosecution is this journal now?" asked the Defense.

"Perhaps we'll find out once the Defense decides to give us some information about the whereabouts of the defendant's wife!" replied the Prosecutor.

The Judge tapped on the table. "Defendant, you can see"—the Judge himself spoke—"that your silence leads not only to fruitless debate, it argues against you."

"I am asked too many things at once, your Honor, and no matter how I answer, I'm not believed. My wife never came downstairs in her stocking feet, nor have I ever kept a journal. What could I have kept a journal about? Nothing ever happened. I might even go so far as to say the reverse. My wife cried because nothing was happening, and . . . Yes, and because she could no longer bear it. And it is scarcely possible for any of us to bear it. But the situation was beyond changing, it was too late."

Could he explain to the Court exactly what he meant by "nothing happening" and "too late"?

He only meant that naturally one longed for the days when something still happened. Only it was dangerous to give in to this longing, and not just for oneself; for the others, too. It was rather as though one approached a table where three people were playing cards. From farther away one thought: "How nice, they're really playing." The cards slapped the table audibly, the players joked with one another and laughed, they were completely wrapped up in their game. One would like to join in. But just try to get close enough to touch them, or even close enough for them to feel the air in the room displaced, they stop in their tracks. Hands full of cards resting stiffly in mid-air, they stare into the pallor of one another's faces with open mouths—just like a wax museum, or the soldiers in Sleeping Beauty—as though they were asking: "What made us play?" It really was unbearable; especially the first time it happened, it scared one to death. One really hadn't meant to disturb, much less paralyze anyone. It didn't matter whether it was in the office or on the train or in a restaurant; anywhere people were engaged in conversation. As long as they didn't realize they were being listened to, everything seemed natural, important to them. But as soon as they noticed, they ran out of words, or talked too loud in an attempt to overcome their embarrassment. One should never allow this to happen; a sense of shame can kill a man; it can also lead to murder.

"What does all that have to do with this case?" asked the Judge.

"With me, too, it's been touch and go whether I'd die of shame," the defendant almost whispered, but articulating precisely. "That's how I know this danger. Nothing but a mortal melancholy remained to keep my heart beating. Sometimes it actually skipped a beat and that seemed the solution, until I called to my heart—but not so loud, gentlemen; something like this, one doesn't call out loud enough for anyone listening at the door to hear—calling: 'How can you deny yourself the one sustenance that's made for you, from which you could derive such strength that no other confirmation would be necessary?' Such hours are terrifying. We can hardly expect of others what we can scarce bear ourselves. Pardon me, I have no right to burden you with my troubles. That was not my intention."

"What was your intention?"

"I would have no man bewildered by my presence . . . I tried to warn the Court of this possibility from the beginning."

"Please leave that decision to us," said the Judge.

"Besides, it is not a question of the Court; *you* are in question, and the question is: Where is your wife? And, in any case, we will have to content ourselves with the answer, however improbable, that during those night hours you did—nothing. No, please, we are *not* going to argue about words. You sat there, then, and, shall we say, waited. Do you consider waiting so meritorious?"

"Meritorious? No. Necessary."

"Fine, you may be right. But for what? What were you waiting for?"

"For nothing in particular, as I've already said. It is only a chance, nothing more. Perhaps the only chance we have."

"Once more it is my duty," said the Judge, "to put it crassly. You were waiting for 'nothing in particular'; be that as it may, the outcome of your incomprehensible behavior was your wife's disappearance without a trace. Or are you going to contest a causal relation between what you call your 'waiting' and her disappearance?"

"You ask too much," said the defendant.

"Very well, I will try another question. But please do not laugh at my repeated use of an expression you yourself are the author of—the situation is far too serious. Were you, or do you now feel that you were, already in the uninsurable *before* that evening?"

"Yes, evidently," answered the defendant hesitantly. "Yet, the person who's just come into it is the least likely to notice. Others become aware of his fix much more quickly."

"What gives it away?" asked the Judge.

"What could it be? Perhaps a scent . . . Or, rather, the lack of a scent . . ." No, he hadn't intended that as a joke, because really people do begin by sniffing about in astonishment: 'Where's he gotten to? He was here a minute ago and I was on the point of gobbling him up.' But because they'd begun to sniff the air they hit on something else, which diverted them and once more the danger had passed."

"What danger?"

"The danger of being bitten and having to bite back."

"Did you use this strategy of, shall we say, evasion against your wife, too?" asked the Judge, raising his voice a little to cut through the suppressed giggling that filled the courtroom.

"Both of us were very cautious," answered the defendant. "We had to be very cautious. We were living through a sort of probationary period, we knew that. It could be revoked at any moment. Unlike other people, we had no right to dreams."

"And it had been like that from the very beginning?" asked the Judge, shaking his head.

"But I tried to describe that beginning to you. Was that a beginning?"

"And all the same . . ."

"Yes, all the same!" The defendant had almost

shouted. "Or should I say, 'For that very reason'?
And if I am not mistaken, the subject under discussion is usually designated love. And as far as I know,
the feeling that it may not last is a proof of its au-
thenticity."

"How dare you take this tone with us!" the Judge
scolded. "We did not ask you for instruction."

By way of an excuse the defendant said, "It isn't
me, it's my wife! I cannot stand her being attacked
after the fact, when she cannot defend herself. Yes, it
is she you're attacking, and not me. She's being reproached for her disappearance without a trace and
also for her marriage, because on the face of it we
don't seem to have been what the Court considers
happy. What disdain the Court shows for my wife
and every other wife! I lived seven years with her,
and never very far from annihilation. Coming from
near-annihilation and aware of it day and night,
without any security against it. The reason why I've
spoken at such length here, and in words that have
made the Court indignant, has to do perhaps with my
proximity to the realm of the unbearable. Your
Honor, please believe me when I tell you that I, too,
am deeply shaken by the realization, however temporary it may prove to be, that nothing remains of seven
years of a shared life but a crumpled handkerchief
that yields up a few tears, but only to chemical analysis.

"And, in any case, may I make a plea that this

handkerchief be returned to me at the end of the hearing?"

That plea would have to be considered later, the Judge said. If neither of the other gentlemen had any remarks to make, he would like to proceed.

Yes, the Prosecution had something to say. He would like to know if the defendant had ever discussed his views with anyone else. No? That was too bad. Although he was the attorney for the prosecution, he couldn't help pointing out to his colleague that, under certain circumstances, people with whom the defendant had talked about his problem before the event might be useful as witnesses for the defense.

His client had no need of such witnesses, the Defense replied.

But they would simplify matters, the Prosecutor said. Be that as it may, to get back to the point, he'd like to ask the defendant if he didn't feel that he might not be the only one who was acquainted with the uninsurable?

Those who were aware of it were not very numerous.

And of those who were aware—had the defendant ever met any of them?

No, they weren't especially sociable.

Indeed, how revealing! But they resembled each other closely?

They differed very markedly from everyone else.

Ah, so that's how it was. But that was how one recognized them, wasn't it?

One recognized them because one felt alone in their company.

Ah, and that was of course fatal.

Yes, he had chosen the right word that time.

But why don't these uninsurable types speak to each other? That would seem the simplest remedy for their loneliness.

What would they have to speak about?

Well, the experiences they had had, for instance, in that uninsurable realm closed to ordinary mortals.

No, that would be impossible.

What would? Not even among people of the same persuasion?

One simply endured those experiences. And their language was silence.

Aha! So the brethren understood each other's silence? "But how is it, defendant," cried the Prosecutor, "that if this secret society has sworn itself to secrecy you talk about it here?"

"You are mistaken, Mr. Attorney, I am not talking *about* it, I am answering questions put to me by a Court which I have agreed to help to the full extent of my powers. If between answers a bit of silence has penetrated this courtroom, I could not prevent it; the danger isn't easily avoided."

"What danger?"

"The danger words themselves face of devaluation and collapse."

"Or of disappearance without a trace?"

"That, too, Mr. Attorney. We must proceed cautiously."

"If I understand you correctly and have translated your meaning into our ordinary language, you will readily admit that your silence was a danger for your wife."

"Yes, I admit that."

"A grave danger?"

"Yes, you might say so."

"Perhaps even a mortal danger?"

"Precisely."

"Thank you. That will do," the Prosecution said.

The Defense jumped up to protest against these methods. His client had been tricked into giving answers that he understood one way and the Court another. It should have become clear to everyone during this hearing that when his client spoke of danger, even of mortal danger, he meant something quite different from what the law understood by these words. Therefore, the Defense requested that the Court forbid any more of this juggling with words: it only served the Prosecution to create a climate unfavorable to the defendant.

The Judge felt that if anyone had to be reproached for juggling words it was his client. Besides, he was going to ask the defendant to please define what "mortal danger" meant as the words were used by him.

Just as he had done once or twice before, the defendant looked around the courtroom as though seeking assistance. Whenever he did this, those present lost their nerve. Spectators were to be seen turning to their neighbors quickly as though to avoid the defendant's eyes. Others shifted on their chairs or picked at their clothes.

He hadn't asked for this trial, he remarked finally.

He wasn't answering the question, said the Judge.

What question?

The question what he meant by the "mortal danger" his wife had been in.

There was nothing more to say, answered the defendant. All had been said.

The Prosecution asked for the floor. Perhaps, in that case, he could help the defendant; that is, help him explain the words whose meaning was disputed. "Tell us, are you given to sudden anger?"

"Sudden anger? Me?" asked the defendant, astonished.

"Yes, that's what I said. Or let us put it this way: Are you inclined to sudden outbursts of temper?"

"What makes you ask?"

"My god, it's only a simple question! Do I have your permission?"

"Yes, but it's odd all the same."

"It may well be that the Court, too, asks 'odd questions.' It depends on your answer."

"I believe I am correct in answering your question in the negative," answered the defendant. His voice was full of distrust. "If you were to ask the people with whom I have done business over the years, I believe you would find my answer fully borne out. Probably you would hear me described as a very quiet and exceedingly reserved person, a man who gets out of trouble's way and who, when a disagreement arises, quickly gives in, to smooth things over. The qualification 'dependable,' which has been given me, should suffice to settle the Prosecution's question."

"Admitted, but perhaps that only tells us something about your really admirable self-control. Indeed, your invoking of testimony by people whom you obviously have no high opinion of, and your refraining from direct personal comment of your own, allows us to infer that you might be given to sudden outbursts. A suspicion, in any case . . ."

"Suspicion?"

"Yes, indeed, the suspicion has not been refuted. It could be, for instance, that you fear the repetition of these outbursts, or perhaps only their outcome, because you have had many unpleasant experiences of this nature, and for this reason you have dammed up your rage, but still aren't really free of it."

"Who told you all this?" asked the defendant.

"Is your answer to be taken as an admission of the accuracy of my suspicion?" the Prosecutor asked suddenly.

"If you insist on knowing the whole story: within limits, yes. That is to say, the designation 'sudden anger' isn't exactly right perhaps, but I confess that I am very vulnerable, and since I am aware of this, naturally I do what I can to protect myself from inadvertent contact, as best I can at least; so as not to cry out in pain."

The defendant had said this calmly and as if smiling to his secret self. But the Prosecution understood it in the sense of the question. "Thank you!" he snapped and then turned immediately to the Court. "The reason for my question will be found in these papers here. And, indeed, it was the defendant's mother—"

"My mother?" The defendant was startled.

"You are only to speak when spoken to," said the Judge.

"His mother declared before the examining magistrate," the Prosecutor continued, "that as a boy the defendant tended to dangerous outbursts of temper. It was never predictable, nor were there ever valid grounds—assuming for the moment that a child ever has them for such behavior! She could always see it coming, though, because her son would suddenly go pale as death, particularly on the tip of his nose. Then she was actually afraid of him. I felt the Court should know about this."

The Defense asked to speak. It gave the proceedings a rather comic turn—the Prosecution's emphasis on the declarations of this old woman! With all due respect to the old lady, he'd like to suggest the possibility that she felt flattered by this whole business, and to prolong this welcome conversation and give the impression that she was indispensable had blabbed out the most trivial things—which the examining magistrate had turned into official documents, only to have them improperly evaluated by the Prosecution. In any case, an accusation must be rather flimsily based when the only witness for the prosecution was the defendant's own mother.

The Defense, too, had a chance to call the defendant's mother as a witness, rejoined the Prosecution. Mothers were usually witnesses for the defense.

The Judge's tapping on the table put an end to this exchange between Prosecution and Defense. "Do you have anything to add?" the Judge asked the defendant.

As for him, he had stood there all the while just as pale as in his mother's description of him before a tantrum when he was a boy. And this time, too, he did not seem to be fully in control.

"A mother is always right," he muttered hoarsely

to himself, and so low that only the stenographer caught it—and only by chance.

"Louder, please!" the Judge exhorted. "What was that?"

"I said, all is lost if I should defend myself against my own mother."

"How are we to take that?"

"Why is she trying to do me injury? It simply passeth understanding. I'm defenseless."

"I only asked you if what your mother told us is true."

"Did she by any chance also tell the examining magistrate the reason why as a child I was given to outbursts of what we are calling 'sudden anger' here? I almost died of it. You would think that as a mother she would have had more fear *for* me than, as she now states, *of* me."

"You have already heard that she said there was never a good reason."

"Then . . . Then . . . Then let us suppose that she has forgotten the reason. She's fortunate. God forbid we should awaken the memory in her! My brother died from it before his time; his blood simply curdled. And me? What has become of me? But she never knew anything about it. It was instinct rather than a guilty choice. Let us leave it at that."

"In your opinion, then, there were valid reasons?"

"The reasons have always escaped me, your Honor.

My mother has an unerring sense of other people's raw nerves. And she cannot resist the pleasure of touching them. This produces a sort of short circuit. Please ask me no more about it. She is my mother all the same, and I am not free from all the feelings and longings connected with that word. Notwithstanding, my mother is not a suitable witness."

"Nor do I give much weight to her testimony," interjected the Prosecutor. "But I have another question. Did your *wife* touch this raw nerve you have spoken of?"

"My wife? I find it really insulting that you should cast ill on my wife by naming her in the same breath as my mother. Is there no way of stopping this, your Honor?"

"You can refuse to answer at any time," was the reply.

"But it's my wife who's at stake, not I. My wife was as aware of it in me, just as clearly as I was aware of it in her, that we were missing or perhaps had lost a layer of skin which other people don't even notice they have, it's so natural. We had to be as careful as hemophiliacs, who don't dare bump into anything, not even into one another. Therefore, neither could let the other out of his sight, for we had to be on guard for the slightest change of tone, if we were to act in time to prevent the other's getting lost. We didn't dare risk a backward look to our origins or to the terrors of childhood; we didn't even dare consider them, since that would have made us dizzy and we would have seen each other only as though in a haze. But there is sleep, gentlemen. Who among us can boast that he is lord over the wind which blows there or can protect himself from it? One is swept first here, then there, from one region into another, forward and backward in time, sucked up lighter than a feather into the thin light, but blinded with gazing; heavy as a hundred pounds of dead weight, growing heavier and heavier, then faster and faster one plummets through the fog until one reaches the surface of some body of water and breaks it—what pain cries out!—then sinks downward toward the horrifying eternity of the carnivorous flowers. Gentlemen, what is one to do when one lies awake next to someone and sees all this and hears the cry, the whimpering? What's the use of one's saying: 'It's all a dream, it only lasts seconds'? Oh, one knows there's a life there in which one has no part, and one feels betrayed and degraded, unable to take part. And even if one does not notice this when it is happening, one can't help but do so the next morning; for the dreamer awakened gives off a strange scent, or is it a shimmer obscuring the outline? Is there any way to hide that? One tries to wash it away, one rushes in to shave, one puts on one's clothes, there's breakfast to fix in the kitchen, lies, lies; there's been a betrayal and there's no certainty any more. Everything is only a pretext, only a respite. What a victory over myself it is, night

after night, just forcing myself to lie down and sleep.
Not until I had exhausted every possibility to the
point where it had lost all power to tempt me, not
until then did I acquiesce to the hazard of sleep. But
earlier, while awake, I exposed myself to all possible
dangers—but who can know them all? Yes, that may
have been my mistake, that I became too used to
them, even laughed at them—yes, in that state no
one was allowed to call me: at the slightest touch, I
would have burst—like a soap bubble. Nothing
would have been left of me but a few biting drops
squirted into the other's eyes. Yes, I overrated my
strength, that's why I'm here."

"If I have understood you correctly," probed the
Judge, "you mean that this soap bubble, as you call
it, burst that very night?"

"Yes, if you say so; that's one way of putting it."

"And it burst from the untimely touch of your wife,
didn't it?"

"Untimely? It was nothing more nor less than her
prerogative if she couldn't stand it any longer!"

"It had gone so far she couldn't stand it any
longer?"

"Perhaps she noticed how my resistance was weak-
ening, that is, before I became aware of it myself. I
wanted to prevent it, yes, I thought I could slow it
down by going away with her. Originally I never
even considered such a move—held it for impossible,

actually—until I suddenly turned to her with 'Good, let's go! Let's go! What more can happen to us? Nothing can touch us now. We can go wherever we please, be it filth, misery, sin . . . They can violate us, they can let us starve, they can mock us and maim us, they can send us to prison . . .'

"Yes, gentlemen, why don't you just send me to prison? For life, I don't care. Why all this trouble beforehand, all these painful words? You know nothing I say is in order here. Forgive me."

"And when did you say that to your wife?" asked the Judge, but in no way showing his astonishment at this outburst of the defendant's.

"When? What do you mean *when*? At the last moment, of course; when it was too late."

"Oh yes, I see. When your wife got to the bottom of the stairs, was it? That was the moment of the greatest danger, as you say."

"It was horrible," said the defendant.

As if in play, the Judge touched his lips with his pencil, to indicate to the Prosecution that this was not the moment to disturb the defendant, who seemed ready now to testify. In vain! Did the defendant notice or did he regain his composure because of something else? In any case, he surprised the Court by remarking suddenly: "How guileful you are, gentlemen! You have enticed words from me that have nothing to do with the business in hand. Words which may never have been spoken . . . Now suppose I only thought them . . . Who can prove it one way or the other?" His voice was almost gay.

On the whole, the defendant's sudden about-face seemed to make a poor impression. It made him less credible, he now lay open to the suspicion that he was merely a clever actor, one who was well aware of the effects he was creating. The public was caught in a clear case of nerves.

"Defendant, you are mistaken," said the Judge. "Everything which relates to your married life is in order here. What we heard from you a few minutes ago goes back to that moment when late at night your wife reached the bottom of the steps, does it not? We have no wish to delve further at present. For all that, I should like to anticipate slightly with the following question. You have called that moment 'horrible'; you have made repeated use of the words 'mortal danger.' Those are strong expressions and lead us to think of even worse ones . . . The reason we do this is that we still do not understand what else you could mean by them. And to evade this 'mortal danger,' according to your own account, you reached the decision to depart with your wife, where to we don't yet know—nor does this seem to have been your original intention. Please do not interrupt; we will return to this point. There's something quite different which I now want to know. Why did you feel that you had to go *out* with her? Wouldn't it have been easier simply to go upstairs?"

"Upstairs? You mean to bed?" cried the defendant.

"Of course. It is certainly most unusual to go out around midnight, on the spur of the moment, and without any definite goal."

"Are you serious?"

"Defendant, when will this finally be clear to you? The Court is no place for jokes! Will you please answer my question."

"No, it's impossible."

"What? You cannot answer?"

"It was impossible to go upstairs . . ."

"Buy why? Now think a minute. Just suppose you had gone upstairs with her. What would have happened?"

"It would have meant the end," said the defendant.

"The end? The end of what?"

"How can anyone ask me such questions?"

"I really don't see what could seem strange to you about this question. To all of us here, it seems the most natural question in the world. And all the more reason to ask it, since in our opinion your wife's disappearance could have been prevented if you had simply gone upstairs with her. There just has to be some reason which you are keeping from us. Or is it rather that your wife would have refused or tried to defend herself?"

152

"Even if she hadn't defended herself . . ."

"Then she did defend herself?"

"She did not!" cried out the defendant. "She did not need to defend herself! Against me? Can you believe I would make such shameless demands upon my own wife?"

"What do you mean, shameless? What sort of word is that to qualify behavior which seems natural to all of us, or in any case more natural than the behavior you showed at the time. Words like that, and then this reiterated 'mortal danger' . . . Yes, what *can* you mean by 'mortal danger'? Your wife came down the stairs. Admittedly at an unusual hour. You were frightened, so. You might even have been 'very frightened,' since you weren't prepared for it. But none of that gives you the right to talk about mortal danger. There must be something missing in your account. If I try to picture the scene . . ."

The Judge was interrupted by an embarrassing incident. And for this reason the defendant had no chance to answer; that is, even if he had wanted to . . .

In the courtroom, indeed in its very center, someone started laughing. A woman. And not at all quietly or as though trying to restrain herself; no, it was immediate and strident. Perhaps she had been suppressing her laughter for some time. The public winced as if it had been whipped. All eyes looked her way. The Judge was about to reach for his bell when his hand stopped in mid-air and sank to the table. It was perfectly evident that this obtrusive laughter was hysteria pure and simple. The people sitting near the woman did what they could to quiet her. Ushers and Court personnel pushed their way to her seat. People sitting in the same row got up to let the woman by. Nor did she try to defend herself; she just let them lead her out. But she didn't stop laughing for a minute; the bursts came in shorter and shorter intervals and could still be heard even after the courtroom door had closed behind her, until at last they faded out in the long corridors outside. Even then, everyone was still listening for this laughter, as though it had only crept into a corner and could flare up again at any minute.

The only person who had not turned in the direction of this hubbub was the defendant. During the whole incident, he simply stood there, quite still, his head bowed slightly, staring at the floor.

The Judge turned to the Assessors and whispered with them. Apparently he was discussing whether the Court should be recessed for a while. Then an official appeared, spoke softly to the Judge, and handed him a memorandum. The Judge read this memorandum, then had it passed to the Prosecutor, who read it also and shrugged his shoulders. At this point the Judge grabbed the bell.

"Order in the Court!" he cried. "Otherwise I shall have to continue behind closed doors." Then he motioned the defendant over and showed him the memorandum. "Is this lady, or her name at least, known to you?" he asked. His discretion prevented him naming the lady publicly.

The defendant shook his head.

"Good. We will check that, of course," said the Judge. "The hearing will proceed."

A controversy between Defense and Prosecution developed. The Defense took advantage of the hysteria of the unknown spectator to declare that the ladies present at the hearing had a better understanding of the ineffable tensions in his client's marriage than the Court had. The Prosecution derided this. If the Defense were to make an appeal to the ladies, the Prosecution would have to rise to the occasion by doing the same, but he would have to ask them if they would be agreeable to disappearing without a trace from their present existences.

It isn't necessary to repeat this controversy in detail. Its principal result was to make everyone forget the previous incident. Presently the Judge tapped on the table with his pencil and warned the disputants to stick to the subject. The Prosecutor asked that he be allowed to ask one pertinent question. "Tell us, defendant, was it your intention to share your wife's death?"

No, it had never been his intention to share his wife's death.

"Why do you answer by repeating my words like that?"

He had only answered as he had been questioned.

"Does that mean that, like me, you lay the accent on the word *share?*"

It meant that in his life, as in that of his wife, there had been no place for romantic notions. For mistakes perhaps, mistakes caused by fatigue, he meant—no one was perfect.

"Your wife never suggested the possibility of your dying together, then?"

"No, why should she have?"

"Not even that night?"

"Not even that night. She didn't need to."

"How's that? What do you mean by that?"

"By that I mean exactly what I said: she didn't need to. Death was with us, between us, around us, and we both knew it. We didn't have to talk about it."

"How am I to understand that?"

"I don't see that there is anything about it you could fail to understand. Really it was more a question of deciding to share *life*, but that too was so clear to both of us that an invitation would have sounded silly."

"But it doesn't seem to have been all that clear, because, although you are standing here before us, your wife has disappeared without a trace. And as for you, what state are you really in? Have you never, how shall we put it, reckoned with death?"

Hadn't he been an insurance agent, the defendant wanted to know. (This answer excited a certain amount of merriment. The Judge had to call the public to order.)

"You have mistaken my meaning," said the Prosecutor. "I want to know if you have ever wanted to end your own life."

"Perhaps earlier."

"Earlier?"

"Before I took that long train ride. I have already attempted to describe that for you. It almost seems to me that your only grounds for suspicion were the size of my insurance policy."

"That never occurred to me," admitted the Prosecutor. "But you are right; your life insurance, too, speaks in its favor. Very well, you claim never to have had such ideas again, after you married. But how does that gibe with the rest of your testimony?"

"Which part?"

"Your whole testimony suggests that you had always planned to 'depart,' as you say, 'into the uninsurable' alone, leaving your wife behind somehow."

"That is correct," confessed the defendant. He had never said he was free of masculine arrogance.

"Now what does that mean?"

It meant that he had been arrogant in presuming that it wouldn't do to expose a woman to uncertainty, and therefore, by taking precautionary measures, abandon her to a way of life which one rejected oneself. He had considered his wife too weak, and it had turned out that he was the weak one. "I used to believe she would inhibit me. I did not trust myself to be stronger than that inhibition. My weakness could so easily have turned to hate. That's what I feared. Yes, I was afraid of that moment of horror."

"Moment of horror?"

"Yes, you could call it that."

"Do you mean by that the moment when your wife reached the foot of the stairs?"

"Yes, that was one of those moments. In any case, I was frightened, very frightened. And I behaved so badly. But that has no place here. I only mentioned it because it is one of the reasons why I will accept your condemnation."

Every time the defendant anticipated his condemnation in this way, an embarrassed pause followed. This time it allowed the defendant to proceed quietly: "I have already asked my counsel . . ."

"What was that?" asked the Judge as if frightened.

"I have asked my counsel already if there wasn't . . ."

"You will have to speak louder!"

"He said there was no such law, but in my opinion there should be."

"What law?"

"Whenever anyone, either through weakness or

through refined hesitation, manages to make another person cry or feel guilty, that must be designated a dangerous form of cruelty and punished as such. If you can establish that in this respect, gentlemen, I am a true son of my mother, even though I feel that I have done everything possible not to become such a one, then . . . But there is no such law."

"What did your wife have to feel guilty about?" asked the Judge.

"It might have been nothing more than a passing mood. How would I know?" said the defendant.

At this point the Prosecution came in again. The Judge had motioned to him with a nod of his head. "Tell us, do you believe it possible that your wife discussed her marriage with someone?"

"Someone?"

"Well, yes, a friend, male or female."

"We had no friends."

"That applies to your wife, too?"

"In order for me to answer your question, you must allow me to rephrase it, to bring out what you really mean, Mr. Attorney. You are asking me whether my wife left me for another man, right? Why not call a spade a spade? Do you consider me too much of a prude? Or too possessive? By the way, the counsel the Court appointed to defend me even suggested that possibility to me! And you're perfectly right. Why not? My wife is still young and very good-looking."

"Defendant!" warned the Judge.

"Excuse me! But I was asked . . . Unfortunately, my answer will disappoint you. For I maintain that it is the duty of the Court to prove the existence of this other man; it is not mine. And until you have found him—even though he turn out to be an angel—you can hold me hostage."

For his disdainful answer the Judge once more called the defendant to order. As the Prosecution had no further questions, the Judge proceeded with the hearing. "Let us now concern ourselves with the moment your wife descended the stairs." The illumination of this situation required a most detailed exposition. The most trivial particulars could be important. According to the account the defendant had given, he had been in the kitchen emptying an ashtray when he heard something. "What did you hear?"

"The door to our bedroom, or perhaps it was the floorboards on the first floor."

"Did you know immediately that it was your wife?"

"Who else could it have been?"

"Well, the maid, for instance."

"The maid? No, I knew immediately."

"Could that be because you had reckoned on your wife's coming downstairs?"

"It couldn't have been anyone else."

"Very well. How did you react?"

"I listened."

"Had you already emptied the ashtray?"

"Yes, I believe so. But how would I remember that?"

"But it was still in your hand?"

"That is possible. Why are you so interested in this ashtray?"

"And next, what happened next? What did you do?"

"Nothing at all. All the blood left my heart. It skipped a beat. I felt as though I'd been caught in the act."

"But why did you? You weren't doing anything wrong? Not even anything out of the ordinary?"

"My mistake was in being so *far away*. I had forgotten to return promptly . . . I wasn't yet awake again."

"Very well, what next?"

"I heard her coming down the stairs. Very slowly, or so it seemed. And it still seems so today, though it can't really have lasted very long. Then I could see her. First her shoes and then her legs."

"From the kitchen?"

"Yes."

"From where you were emptying the ashtray, the stairs are not visible."

"Then I must have walked to the kitchen door without even knowing it. Yes, that's how it had to be. I leaned against the doorpost. It would have been impossible to move. I even thought I couldn't be seen from there."

"How's that? How did you come to think that?"

"I don't know. This is like a gap . . ."

"In your memory?"

"No, not in my memory. I mean the kitchen door, a gap open on emptiness."

"Very well. And then you regained control of yourself?"

"Regained control?"

"Or you got a grip on yourself again?"

"Oh, we only talk like that after it's all over. It's mere boasting."

"What did you think at the time?"

"Nothing, your Honor. Believe me, in moments like that, no one *thinks*. It wouldn't mean anything; and no one is capable of it. One acts."

"How did you act?"

"I gave up. I gave in."

"Whom did you give in to? Or what did you give up?"

"Whom? What?" stammered the defendant.

"Did you give in to your wife?"

"How could it be her? No, not her . . ."

"Your words must mean something!"

"I gave up all resistance. It was simply no longer possible, this continuous resistance. It was too late for that. I just let myself drift. Otherwise . . ."

"Otherwise?"

"I have no idea what would have happened 'otherwise.' It is beyond thinking about."

"You reached a sort of decision then?"

"But I've already explained that there wasn't a drop of blood left in my brain! You can't talk about a decision in a case like this. I had to lean against the doorpost."

"And your wife?"

"What do you mean? How does she come into it?"

"Did she notice the state you were in?"

"How would I know? Yes, of course she would have noticed it. I mean, she might have been in the same state."

"Very well. But let us stop a moment to consider what you have told us. Now you were standing in the open kitchen door, leaning against the doorpost. On the right or on the left?"

"On . . . On . . . Isn't that completely irrelevant?"

"Would you please allow us to be the judge of that?"

"I really haven't the least notion any longer. It seems to me that it was on the left. But perhaps I wasn't leaning at all—it only just occurred to me a moment ago that I was."

"Good, let's stick to the left, if that sounds right to you. And where was the ashtray?"

"The ashtray?"

"Yes, you had gone to the kitchen to empty it, and a few moments ago you told us that you had just emptied it. So that ashtray had to be somewhere . . ."

"Weren't you able to locate it?"

"That is what we are asking you to do."

"But it has to be there. I must have left it by the kitchen sink. Or on the kitchen table. Perhaps the maid . . . What does the ashtray matter?"

"Good. You put it aside to leave your hands free. Which ashtray had you used that evening?"

"Which? The one that's always in the living room. It's always the same one."

"Describe it to us, please."

"A big ashtray. My wife never liked it. She said I ought to take it to the office, that's where it belonged. But with those smaller ashtrays she bought to replace it, ashes were always falling on the table—so it stayed. It was marble, greenish. You can buy them anywhere."

"So it was a rather heavy object?"

"Yes. My wife had glued some felt to the bottom so it wouldn't scratch the table."

"Was it round?"

"No, six- or eight-sided, with sharp edges."

"How heavy, approximately?"

"How heavy? Who ever weighs an ashtray? A pound or two, perhaps. Nearer two pounds, I believe."

"Very well. How are we to explain this ashtray's being picked up on the fourth step of the staircase, and indeed very near the banister?"

"On the fourth . . . Then why did you ask me

all those questions? There it is! Everything's fine!"

"But you said only a few minutes ago that you left it in the kitchen."

"But it's the same, either way. I must have had it in my hand still and put it down on that step to be rid of it. That shows you how little time I had for such details."

"Hmmm. And when did you put it on that step?"

"When? My god, what questions! Some time or other. I fail to see . . ."

"We, too, 'fail to see' . . . For example, we fail to see why you have just contradicted yourself."

"Your Honor, all this time I have been trying to make it clear that this was a matter of life and death. How is one to keep track of something so laughably insignificant as an ashtray at a time like this?"

"So you felt your life threatened by your wife?"

"By my . . . How repugnant all this is! It would be best if I said nothing more. Everything I've said has been misconstrued, purposely."

"In any case, there seems to be no disagreement about one thing. You still had that ashtray in your hand when your wife came down the stairs."

"Yes, why not? The detail is irrelevant."

"You wouldn't happen to recall whether your wife was still on the stairs or already in the hall when you put that ashtray down, would you?"

"No. I mean . . ."

"Yes?"

"Why do you want to know?"

"It may have been only a second, or it may have been a tenth of a second. But you yourself spoke of a 'second of horror.' It is the Court's business to understand what you meant by that."

The Judge's tone had been matter-of-fact, with no special emphasis. He glanced indifferently at the defendant, who seemed on the verge of answering, without hesitation, as he had done so far. His mouth was open—when suddenly he stopped and turned white as chalk. People were afraid he might faint.

But nothing of the kind happened. Slowly, as though in a dream, and as though he had forgotten where he was, he walked over to the table at which the Judge sat (and the Judge did not try to stop him) and, supporting himself with both hands, bent over as far as he could and asked, more in a hiss than out loud: "Has she been found?"

We can scarcely assume that this question was overheard by the public; nevertheless, tension spread through the chamber. Everyone seemed to think some decisive admission had been made, and the very fact that no one had heard it increased the general restlessness. People turned to each other with inquiring looks, some cupped a hand behind an ear. It seemed as though at any moment a voice in the crowd would shout, "Louder please!"

The Defense jumped up to rush to his client's assistance, but the Judge waved him away. "Just a moment, Counsel, you may speak in a moment." Yet this slight interruption seemed welcome to his Honor. Calmly, in an almost fatherly tone, he turned to the defendant. "I don't believe I understood your question."

"It's impossible," said the defendant.

"What is impossible?"

"I left the house with her and it was only in that snowstorm I lost sight of her. And you can suggest that I struck her dead with that ashtray? It cannot be. Then it couldn't have been me. For I . . . And if someone has found her, why wasn't I told from the very beginning? What has been the point of this torture here?"

"Now keep calm, defendant. We . . ."

"Well, where did you find her then?" cried out the defendant.

"Your wife has not been found."

"Then what's the meaning of all this about an ashtray?"

As a matter of fact, the defendant did return to his place, but not without violently shaking his head and addressing the public: "I'm being mocked here . . ."

The Defense took exception to the method employed by the Court: his client had been tormented with a suspicion which the Court already knew to be completely groundless. (He even let fall the phrase "medieval methods.")

The Judge replied, by way of an excuse, that due

to the unusual nature of the business at hand it had seemed wise to establish, by whatever means, the defendant's psychic susceptibility to the performance of a deed of violence, since the very evasion of such a deed might well throw light on what followed.

If it were a question of "psychic susceptibility," mused the Defense, there would hardly be a man alive— ("Who would go free," or something like that; he had obviously intended to complete his remark thus, but his client interrupted.)

"And to think that I almost believed you!" said the defendant to the Judge, reproachfully. "That's no way to behave! You have no right to do things like that."

"Almost?" asked the Judge, not allowing the unseemly conduct of the defendant to ruffle his calm. "Now hear this, if someone were suddenly to tell me that I had—call it what we will—done something to my wife, I would not for a moment 'almost believe it'!"

"In that case, your Honor, you have never been in the state I was in—and am in still. Nothing is certain, absolutely nothing. And words least of all."

The Prosecution came to the Judge's assistance. Could the defendant recall how the staircase had been lighted?

It hadn't been.

Then the light must have been on in the kitchen?

In the kitchen? No, it would never have been. The

switch there snapped on so loud he never touched it at night. And besides, what for? Every step and every movement of the hand had been memorized years before.

"Oh yes, that's very thoughtful . . ." said the Prosecutor. Then presumably the door to the living room had been open, and light from the chandelier . . .

Chandelier? No, that certainly wouldn't have been on. Why such irksome brightness? It only hurt the eyes. His reading lamp, that must have been on.

Oh, so it was the reading lamp. Wouldn't that have been rather weak for lighting the staircase on the other side of the door?

What would he have wanted to light it for?

"Well, for instance, for yourself, so you could tell your wife had cried."

"That's something one can recognize as well in the dark. Even better. No, I cannot free myself of this image of my wife lying there at the foot of the stairs, struck down, struck dead *by me*, and with this silly ashtray. What have you done to me? Yes, and I am standing next to her, bending over. Wouldn't it have been better to have left *that* in the dark? Now for the rest of our life we will have to be careful that this image does not become a reality."

The Defense reproved the Court in a long digression. He maintained that they were attempting, by whatever means, to reconstruct logically a situation that lay outside the confines of logic. By now the

Court should have seen quite clearly that the usual criminal procedures, when applied to his client, led to false results. Even he, counsel for the Defense— and God knows his client hadn't made his job easy— even he, like any experienced lawyer, had at first felt suspicious—where there was smoke, etc. . . . Something was being covered up, and thinking this, he had gone completely astray, had gone in circles just like today's hearing. He had gone on this way until one day he had decided to tackle the problem from precisely the opposite angle. He had assumed that no attempt was being made to hush anything up; on the contrary, his client was doing everything in his power to say more than people usually felt they needed to say, be it in court or in daily life. More, indeed, than speech allowed. Every misunderstanding which had troubled them that day had resulted from his client's endeavor to explain metaphysical realities in physical words. Now, there was no one here, was there, who doubted that the metaphysical (however they might differ in defining it) was more than a mere abstract notion; no, it was something quite real which influenced their physical existence decisively. His client had often enough reiterated his acceptance of the Court and its laws as a defense against the untimely eruption of the metaphysical into society. On the other hand, it was equally clear that the metaphysical could never become the subject of juridical discussion. Yet, all the same, it played a part in the relations between the sexes, at least as a source of tension, which could scarcely be overrated. He was speaking now as counsel for the Defense: he had chosen this example deliberately, as in some barely definable way suited to the matter in hand. Who would be so rash as to suppose he had said the last word about the moment of the sexes' most intimate union? Yes, they all knew the functions of the body and they all thought they knew the course of psychological events, but at bottom these, too, were part of the body only. And out of this knowledge nothing of any validity at all could be said about the moment itself; just something about its prerequisites and its consequences. Obviously, the moment itself eluded consciousness. In the memory a vague impression remained, of happiness, or torment; or even, to be more exact, the impression of a *gap;* yes, a relaxation of the everyday laws of logic and physics. In the course of this hearing, every emergence of this temporary relaxation had been taken for contempt for these very laws; from an absolutist point of view, perhaps. What was a law worth if it were relaxed occasionally, if it must be? Yes, must be! A court which sincerely believed something of that sort would, if it wanted to be consistent, have to indict each man who admitted that for a moment *he hadn't a thought in his head,* because he would have belittled the law in merely forgetting the laws. Presumably such an attitude would lead to existence becoming totally sterile.

He had used the word "gap" on purpose, continued the Defense, because his client had used it. He could just as well have said "second of horror," since that, too, had been said repeatedly—and repeatedly misunderstood. Now, as for this "second of horror"—and couldn't one just as usefully analyze a second of happiness?—of course a man with a stop watch in his hand might very well establish that indeed a second had elapsed, but really didn't all of them know that this instant couldn't be measured by the clock, that actually what one had experienced was an instant outside of time? However one might explain that instant's being "outside of time," its being there was an incontrovertible fact. In any case, that was what he believed his client meant and that was the sense in which he and his testimony would have to be taken to be understood. Now, how one was to evaluate the "uninsurable" instant was another matter. First of all, though, one would have to come to terms with the *fact* of his client's point of view—as it was only fitting that a jurist do. This much, in any case, the Defense would like to see accepted as true beyond argument: that his client, at that moment when his wife unexpectedly came back downstairs, found himself in just such a "gap." The Court might allow that the open kitchen door symbolized this gap in time. "Everything that a jurist can discover about this gap with the help of criminal-case methods," the Defense said, concluding his discourse, "he will end up regarding as outright mystification. But that will be the jurist's own fault since the standpoint from which he has been asking his questions is wrong."

The Prosecution demanded to speak immediately. "If I accept the example proposed by the Defense, it is nonetheless worth remarking that this 'gap' which occurs during the embrace of husband and wife can lead to the conception of children—thus this gap is fruitful—whereas that kitchen door, gap that it is, leads only to the disappearance without a trace of the defendant's wife. This difference seems to me a fact not uninteresting to the jurist."

"It is the business and the duty of the Prosecution to answer like this," mused the Defense.

The Judge thanked the Defense for this discourse, even if it perhaps would have been better saved for his summation. Nonetheless, the Judge had not thought to interrupt, since anything which might shed light on this vexing question was welcome. What he had heard prompted him to ask the following. Did the Defense propose to establish that during that night, or for a moment at the foot of the stairs, the defendant's mind was impaired, and that therefore he could not be held completely responsible for his behavior?

The defendant gesticulated wildly, and his counsel jumped up, quite obviously to get in ahead of him.

He had intended nothing of the kind. On the contrary. "Actually, this is the one point which my client

(who declined my services, considering them super-
fluous) discussed unambiguously with me. Naturally,
I considered it my duty to point out that his way of
answering might easily make the Court question
whether he were of sound mind. Not only did my
client forbid my using this argument in his defense—
which, by the way, had never been my intention. He
made it clear that he would contest the jurisdiction of
any court which placed his sanity in doubt. I was to
appeal immediately to a higher court."

"Strong words, strong words," mused the Judge.

"Of course I informed my client that every judge,
and, under certain circumstances, the Prosecution as
well, has the right to call in experts to verify their
opinions, and that there was no way to prevent this.
Thereupon my client suggested that we do the Court
one better by obtaining the prior certification of his
sanity by consulting with leading psychiatrists. But
this step was never taken, as I advised against it,"
continued the Defense. "It isn't easy to defend someone who rejects not only the counsel for the defense,
but any form of defense at all. I would long ago have
given up this task to which the Court appointed me,
were I not persuaded—no, let us say, were I not absolutely certain, that my client really doesn't need any
defense. And therefore my duty is to clear up a few
misunderstandings which I saw would be unavoid-
able. This whole trial, from beginning to end, has
been a misunderstanding; in that, too, I find myself in

complete agreement with my client. Now to get back to the question of my client's sanity: it isn't so much that he considered any doubt of it an insult, though he very well may; no, what really tips the scales for him is his feeling that in so doubting it the Court only makes itself laughable. I do not feel that I am being indiscreet if I quote my client on this subject. I noted his words down at the time. He said, 'Whoever concludes a pact with psychiatry declares himself bankrupt. Man only begins where psychiatry leaves off.' "

"Come now," said the Judge.

"Just a moment, and I will have had my say. There is one more statement of his that I noted down—it came out during the same conversation. My client expressed this opinion: 'How can a court depend for its understanding of a situation on people who make dreams their business though they are not in a position to stop dreaming themselves, much less have they the strength to live out their dreams.' "

"Come now," said the Judge once again. Then he asked the defendant if he were still of this opinion.

He answered that he was. It was nothing more than a way of frittering time away.

"We aren't here for our pleasure either," said the Judge. "This useless beating around the bush that brings us no nearer to our common goal wearies us as much as it does you."

What more was being asked of him?

"For the time being, nothing more than that you answer all the Court's questions as precisely as possible. Let us proceed. You claim that neither your wife nor you said a word. That is absolutely incomprehensible to us; but very well, let's leave it at that. Continue your narrative. What happened next? What did you do when your wife reached the foot of the stairs, when, judging by the position of the stairs, you must have stood opposite her?"

"I went to the closet and took her winter coat off the hanger."

"Wait a moment! Not so fast. Since the bottom steps project a little into the front hall, it is very narrow there between the door to the kitchen and the door to the living room. So, if you wanted to reach the coat closet, you would have had to squeeze past your wife. Is that how it was?"

"Yes, perhaps."

"Did you rub up against her?"

"How could I know that still? But the door to the living room must have been open . . ."

"So you had gone back into the living room?"

"No, but I could have avoided my wife."

"Fine. You went to the closet. This presumably gave you the opportunity of setting the ashtray—which you were still carrying—down on the edge of the fourth step?"

"Yes, it could have happened like that . . ."

"And your wife really never said a word? Not even,

for example, when she took the coat? Now, if your leaving together hadn't been agreed on beforehand, this action must have surprised her. She must have been at least as surprised as you were when she came back downstairs contrary to habit and so late at night. Or could it all have been agreed on in advance?"

"No, it hadn't been, but it had been a possibility for a long time."

"That sounds incredible."

"Perhaps she did say something, but not out loud; without moving her lips. That's the way a great deal gets said at moments like these. And it's said so rapidly. No one has a memory for these communications, but none is necessary, as you know the words yourself."

"Wouldn't it be a good idea, though, for you to tell them to us?"

"It isn't possible, your Honor. And the words aren't important. Only a man and his wife can hear them; we had been married seven years—others would have called it silence. We both knew the days of grace had ended. What did we still have to discuss?"

"And why did you reach immediately for her winter coat?"

"Because it was hanging there, and because she had to put something on."

"It was only the end of September, the days were still rather warm. Was her coat out of storage?"

"If we went for a walk in the evening, she always threw it over her shoulders—my wife was very sensitive to cold. And down by the lake, it was always cooler in the evening."

"Oh, I see. So you supposed it would be cold there that night as well?"

"I was already *freezing*. The cold had me shivering."

"And you didn't put on a coat?"

"There wasn't time. And I wasn't the one who mattered . . ."

"Do you mean by that that you were concerned only about the effect upon your wife of this supposed drop in temperature?"

"Men like myself are used to it. But 'concerned' isn't the right word. There was nothing to think over . . . Every act acted itself, so to speak. And any of you would have done the same."

"What do you mean by that?"

"You, too, would have helped your wife into her winter coat."

"So you helped her into her winter coat?"

"Well, of course. And she couldn't find one of the sleeves right away, I was holding the coat so clumsily."

"Curious, the way you remember some trivial details with astonishing clarity," said the Judge.

"Which 'trivial detail'?" The defendant sounded surprised.

"I meant that business about the sleeve."

"I could see her face in the mirror on the closet door, that explains my clumsiness."

"I thought you said you hadn't turned on the hall light?"

"You're right; I hadn't."

"But you were able to see your wife's face in the mirror nontheless?"

"A spot of paleness showed, and that's enough."

"And you kept silent still?"

"Neither of us felt up to talking. I just smoothed the back of her coat. What thin shoulders my wife has."

"Really, why do you mention, for the first time, that she has thin shoulders?"

"Because she has."

"Did it come to you perhaps at that particular moment because you felt pity for your wife?"

"Pity? Pity? We had long ago left pity behind us."

"Now there's another of your incomprehensible statements."

"There isn't anything in it to understand. It is a simple statement of fact."

"And supposing you had pitied her?"

"Why on earth should I have pitied her?"

"Well, to put in the simplest terms: because she is a woman."

The defendant smiled. "That almost sounded like

something I might have said." He hadn't meant it sarcastically, but that's the way the Judge took it.

"That smile is quite out of place," he said. "I want you to be perfectly clear about one thing: this Court has the impression—and I believe that I am speaking here for my colleagues—that an unbridgeable gulf of loathing existed between your wife and you, at least on your part. Every word you have so far said could be interpreted as self-praise occasioned by your never having given in to this loathing."

"And you tell me this because I chanced to remark that my wife has thin shoulders?" asked the defendant, and his voice sounded almost gay.

"Exactly."

"It has nothing to do with loathing, any more than it has to do with love. It was simply an observation. I confess it doesn't gibe with the atmosphere in this courtroom." The defendant accompanied these last, hesitant words with another glance around the chamber. And once more he compelled the Court to follow his gaze. As chance would have it, this was the moment the sun chose to break through the gray blanket of clouds that had covered the sky all day. For about as long as it takes to draw two or three long breaths, a broad beam of light shone through the dirty windows; and since the air was thick with motes of dust, the beam looked almost palpable; it moved searchingly over the rows of spectators and died as suddenly as it had come. The defendant turned once more to the Court. "When we were children and our grandmother told us a story with angels in it, we knew exactly what they were and how to behave in their presence. Later, we either forgot it or we hadn't the time, though nothing had changed, really. Still, though, from time to time, thanks to some trivial detail, everything is quite clear. But just for an instant; when one perceives it, it's already slipping away, and nothing will remain but our common sorrow." Once more, the defendant smiled. "Something like that, gentlemen."

The Judge granted the Prosecution the floor. Could the defendant describe that winter coat?

It was brown. Almost fawn. Some variety of imported lamb . . . Rather thick pelts.

And could he by chance recall where this coat had been bought?

Yes, that shop on the corner, Chez . . . Chez . . . The name would be on the bill, but that was in his office. It had been about two years ago.

Could it have been Chez ——— and the Prosecutor named a shop.

Why yes, how did he know?

And would the defendant recognize the coat if it were to turn up?

The defendant wanted to know how it could possibly turn up. He sounded astonished.

"Do you believe that that is completely impossible?" the Prosecution asked quickly.

"But my wife would still need it!"

"Oh, of course, excuse me. Naturally she needs it; since she left, it really has turned winter. But would you be able to identify the coat?"

"Yes. That is, there were many like hers. But the lining would tell. It rustled a little."

"Thank you, that will do for the moment."

"Now what is all this about a coat?" asked the defendant.

The defendant does not have the right to ask questions, the Judge reminded him, not looking up from his papers. It would appear that he was as much in the dark concerning the Prosecutor's questions about the coat. Only after some hesitation, and after allowing the Prosecution more than enough time to ask further questions, did he address the defendant again. His Honor said that they were approaching a point where he considered it his duty to explain the next step in the case before it was discussed. For, from the standpoint of the minutes of the preliminary investigation, they were faced with a problem that as a matter of fact no court in its right mind could entertain without making itself ridiculous. The Defense had repeatedly raised this objection. Up until now, the defendant's behavior had been incomprehensible, or almost incomprehensible, without being completely incredible. Be that as it may, everything had occurred within the limits of the possible. Yet what they were now to examine could not even lay claim to credibility; it could be rejected beforehand as belonging rather in the realm of dreams or fever. For instance, the snowstorm in which the defendant claimed he lost sight of his wife! In this country, snow was not usual in September; moreover, all that was needed was a call to the Weather Bureau to prove that it had not snowed that night. But besides this, there were several points in the defendant's testimony which did not correspond to the findings of the police. The Court had taken it upon itself to clarify all these difficulties. "If the defendant does not retract," continued the Judge, raising his voice, "the Court will have to decide whether it is dealing with deliberate mystification designed to cover up disagreeable events, or whether the mental state of the defendant was such that night that no information can be expected from him which will bear our scrutiny. These are decisions we must aim for."

After a short pause, the Judge continued his exposition. "To begin, let us select a single occurrence. The defendant assures us that after he had helped his wife into her coat, they left together. I am using the words he used. Cross-examined, he stuck to 'left' and 'together.' More precise information was not forthcoming. To the examining magistrate's obvious question: 'Well, where to?' and to his question of just what he meant by 'left,' the defendant replied with unshakable uniformity: 'Simply *left*.' According to his testimony, this 'left' wasn't even necessarily identical with 'out the front door.' And when we reproached him with the fact that the front door had been left open, he claimed that proved nothing. Certainly it is no *proof;* the front door could have been opened in his absence by a third party. But by whom? This third party has left neither footprints nor fingerprints on the brass doorknob, for instance, to prove his existence. The police spared no pains in searching for this possible third party. In any case, it couldn't have been the maid, since she was sleeping the whole time in her room on the first floor and only woke up when the defendant came home with the night watchman. So it really does seem that the defendant left the house with his wife in such a hurry that he overlooked closing the door behind them—and, by the way, the reading lamp was still on in the living room. Or his wife left alone, either before the defendant, or after him. The latter hypothesis begins to seem less than improbable when we consider the questions the defendant put to the night watchman when the latter found him by the lake. We will hear the night watchman's testimony later on. He only walked toward the lake because he thought he heard cries coming from that direction. Right off he asked the defendant: 'Did you call?' to which the defendant replied: 'Yes, I did. Have you seen my wife?' As the night watchman puts it, this question was asked with obvious signs of agitation. At first he thought the defendant was intoxicated: he was staggering visibly. Only later did the suspicion arise that perhaps a crime had been committed. All this took place in the gray hours of early morning, at about 4 a.m., approximately four hours after the defendant claims to have left together with his wife. What happened during these four hours? How did the defendant get to the lake? What was he looking for there?"

After letting this last question die in the air, the Judge turned once more to the defendant. "In this Court we have heard a certain number of your views on life. It is not the business of a court to take a position either for or against. Yet, no matter how much your thinking may differ from ours, you will have to agree with us that it is physically impossible for a living human being to disappear off the face of the earth without leaving a trace. Thus only these alternatives are left: either something happened to your wife or she is hiding. In either case, you must know more than you've told. And your claim that you are *unable* to give any information is unacceptable to us; we are of the opinion, rather, that you do not *wish* to give any. Or would you prefer our taking this 'inability' for temporary amnesia? It can happen, of course, that a man loses his memory for three or four hours due to fainting or shock, but in that case we would have to consult one of those psychiatrists whom you so disdain. The Court would find itself compelled to call in an expert. If it were professionally declared, on the basis of a psychological examination, that you might well be suffering from amnesia, rather than merely simulating it, we would have to consider the question of just how far you could be absolved from responsibility.

"Yes, Defense? But I would be grateful if you would make it as brief as possible."

The Defense objected only to one word, "responsibility." It would be applicable only where a crime had been committed, as was not the case here.

"Good, it is possible that I expressed myself clumsily," admitted the Judge. "There is, by the way, 'responsibility' in the case of omission, too. But this is of no importance now. Because, no matter how we try to get around it, this major question remains: Where is your wife? Assuming that you did suffer a shock— no, let's leave it at that—and that this shock had as its result the extinction, for several hours, of both power of perception and memory, still you can hardly claim that your wife's disappearance stands in some causal relationship to this extinction."

"Oh, but it does, it does!" cried the defendant, to the surprise of all.

"How's that?" asked the Judge.

"Yes, what becomes of a person when one isn't thinking of him? No one knows . . ."

"The other ceases to exist if we forget him? That's over my head."

"Perhaps he does still exist, but strange and unknown."

"Does that apply to your wife, too, now?"

"Yes, definitely. And I'm to blame."

"Hmmm . . . In other words, if you were to leave this courtroom, it might happen that I, now sitting here before you in the flesh, would lose all reality, simply because I suffered the misfortune of being forgotten by you . . . And worse still, I would lose reality not just for myself but for other people as well; for example, for my colleagues here, and for these spectators. Ours is a truly undependable existence."

"What would I know about you, your Honor?" said the defendant.

"Well, for one thing, you know that I am your Judge and that I am deemed capable of deciding your case."

"That isn't enough, if you will forgive my saying so. It was just your question which startled me. Or was that a rhetorical question only?"

"Which question do you have in mind?"

"Whether I will continue to think of you after I have left this chamber. Perhaps you didn't really mean it. It might very well be that I will think of you, only because you asked that question; it is one of those questions which follow one about, which stick to one. A courtroom isn't large enough for such a question; such a question knows no walls, it forces a way through cracks in windows and doors. Like a cloud, it changes shape gradually in the wind. It may be forced to the ground; but if a part remains, even though hardly measurable, just a slight scent, nothing is lost; from that, the whole can be reconstructed."

"Well, we'll leave me out of this," said the Judge with a smirk. Then he shouted at the public: "I expect good behavior!

"In any case, the Court cannot be satisfied with the 'explanation' that your wife's disappearance resulted from an extinction of your memory. It's absurd. And presumptuous besides, if you will permit me this remark. But it is not for presumption that you are here. Once more I ask you: Where is your wife?"

"I don't know," answered the defendant.

"Why is she hiding and why are you covering up for her?"

"Who told you she's hiding?"

"Yes, Mr. Attorney?"

The Prosecutor suggested that he might be in a position to refresh the defendant's memory.

On a sign from the Prosecution, an usher brought in a rather large bundle and placed it on the table at which the Assessors sat. Then he undid the cord and opened up the brown paper, which took up an unexpected amount of space, so that one of the Assessors had to grab for his pencil and other materials, or they would have been swept to the floor.

"I asked you earlier, defendant," the Prosecutor said, "whether you would recognize your wife's winter coat. Would you mind stepping over here and telling us if this is it?" Every eye followed the defendant as he walked to the table and looked at the folded coat. The defendant stroked the fabric, tenderly examining it here and there, then at last lifted the coat from the table and held it before him by the hanger. In so doing, he pulled the wrapping paper off the table. But the defendant did not let this disturb him, he shoved it aside absent-mindedly with his foot. The lining of the coat held his attention. He examined it in different lights and even looked closely at one of the armholes.

Finally he looked up and asked the Prosecution: "Where was this found?"

"So you recognize the coat as the one your wife wore?" was the reply.

"Yes, of course."

"This is the coat she had on that night?"

"She had no other. But what does its being here indicate?"

"That is what we are asking you."

"Asking *me?* I didn't find it!"

"But a few minutes ago you said your wife would still be needing it . . ."

"But of course she needs it still. Unless . . ."

"Well?"

"Perhaps she bought a new coat. But this one is quite good still."

"Did your wife have enough money to buy herself a new coat?"

"Money? What does money have to do with it?"

"Now, I always believed coats don't grow on trees . . . Or do you mean you believe someone is looking after your wife?"

"Someone? Someone?"

"I only brought up a possibility. And there is also the possibility that the coat was simply lost."

"How could she lose this? Let's not talk nonsense."

"No, we wouldn't want to do that, would we?"

"Where did you find this coat?" asked the defendant.

"I don't believe there's any reason to keep that a secret," said the Prosecutor. "The police found it in a secondhand clothing store in M."

"In M. What is she doing in M.?"

"Would either you or your wife have acquaintances there?"

"I've never even been there, just passed through once or twice. And my wife doesn't know anyone there. This is very mysterious."

"Well, this point seems less mysterious than others. The coat turned up in M. two weeks after the . . . after whatever happened. The dealer took it off a peddler's hands, one who has connections with receivers of stolen goods, but he claimed he got the coat from someone he'd never seen before, in a bar. And this was corroborated by the bar's owner, who loaned the fence money. No matter how seriously we take this testimony, there is no way of getting around the fence's alibi for the previous two weeks. He did not leave M. and thus cannot be otherwise implicated in our case. It is regrettable that we cannot retrace the intermediate steps in the coat's history. Once more we are up against one of those celebrated 'gaps.' Or could you aid us? Have you any idea who this unknown could have been?"

The defendant shook his head, but then shouted with sudden joy, "But what are we doing still talking? Isn't that coat proof that my wife is still . . . is still here?"

"That is just the interpretation we expected from you," remarked the Prosecutor. There was satisfaction in his voice. "Unfortunately, this coat tells us nothing definite about your wife's fate. Thank you."

The defendant still held the coat in his hands, as though he didn't know what to do with it. The usher came and took it from him. At first, the defendant did not want to let him have it, considering the coat his personal property. He even glanced up at the Judge, to see whether he could count on his help here. For a minute the defendant's arm remained in the same position as when the coat was still in his hands. Then his arm fell listlessly to his side. But he did not say a word. He appeared to be deep in thought.

The Judge leaned over quite far and asked the defendant in a kind voice why he didn't simply confess why his wife was hiding. That was a very plain question, wasn't it? "Note that I haven't asked you where, because you might not know, actually; I have simply asked you why. And if the answer would embarrass you, I am willing to clear the court."

Was it punishable, then, for a person to disappear without official permission?

"But, defendant, that's just laughable!" At the most, it would then be a matter of transgressing police regulations, regulations concerning registration upon arrival and departure, for instance. And, of course, giving a false name was punishable. But none of that had much gravity, it wasn't what concerned them here. "Or am I to take your question as an admission that you know the reason for your wife's leaving you and going into hiding?"

But the reason was clear enough: otherwise she would have been lost.

"And you can actually pretend that now she is *not* 'lost'?"

"Now she has a chance," answered the defendant calmly.

"Could you speak a little louder?"

"Perhaps she has a chance now."

"Really, defendant, you try our patience; and, if I may say so, my good humor as well. I am greatly overstepping my powers as a judge by speaking to you as I have and by putting answers in your mouth. I have even expressed an opinion; namely, that personally I am by no means convinced that we are faced with a criminal offense. On the other hand, nothing you have said so far has dissuaded me from the belief that you are consciously concealing something from us—no matter how respectable your motive for so doing may be. The Court cannot tolerate being purposely misled in this fashion. Won't you make up your mind once and for all to talk quite openly to me?"

"I'm terribly sorry about all this, your Honor. The misunderstandings, I mean. I'm not concealing a thing; no, it's not that. I believe I have said all there is to say, but perhaps never clearly enough. But again, it's not out of bad faith, it's just . . . I never talked about it before, that's why. I wasn't allowed to talk about it; otherwise . . . Once upon a time I read that men condemned to die break out in a sweat. Under their arms and all over their bodies. I don't know whether it's true, but I can well imagine that it's so. I, too, have sometimes sweated like that; it's very unpleasant. The first time it happened to me, I knew exactly what it was. That was a long time ago

—before I traveled all night to fetch my wife. It happened in a bar, at a sort of regulars' table. In those days I was a white-collar worker. We went to that bar in the evenings, all of us who were employed in the same line of work, other fellows my age. We were all bachelors. We never drank much—we couldn't afford it. We talked and cracked jokes. Nothing unusual, the same as everywhere else—nice young fellows. I joined in with the rest in laughing at their jokes; and, if I forgot to, my neighbor poked me in the ribs and I laughed. They liked me a lot and I liked them a lot. In the summer we went on outings —to go swimming. And when one of us had a birthday he had to stand the others a treat. My birthday, too, was in their books—they'd looked through the company files. I couldn't get out of it and wouldn't have wanted to. So it was on my birthday that this happened for the first time. The waiter had just brought the frankfurters I had ordered for everybody, and mustard and rolls. The rest made a grab for their food, and I wanted to myself, since . . . Now this is very difficult for me to explain, gentlemen. Please pardon me in advance. Suddenly I was no longer hungry. Or rather, I was still hungry, but I could not eat a bite. Something was choking me and I burst out in a sweat. I pushed my plate away with a certain amount of force; it knocked against a beer glass. I turned to the others: 'Eat all you want, I'm not hungry just now,' I said. 'We could even order

more when these are gone . . .' They were of the
opinion that I'd had too much to drink too fast, but
that wasn't it. I understood for the first time that I
was not one of them. Perhaps I still hoped that in the
morning I would feel differently, because I envied
them so. I would gladly have stayed with this job my
whole life—but I was out of luck. I didn't want them
to notice anything, they'd just have felt insulted. It
got so bad that I actually felt sick every time someone stuck out his hand for me to shake. I always expected to see one of them study his in surprise after
he'd shaken mine and then pull his hurriedly away.
They were separated from me as though plate glass
had been installed between us. No, plate glass won't
do—otherwise, they wouldn't have been able to hold
out their hands . . . It was more a sort of vacuum. I
carried it around with me like an invisible shell, at
work, on the street, in a bar. I never wanted to disappoint anyone, but as soon as I tried to break through
this shell of mine, I would begin to tremble, then
break out in a sweat, followed by a chill. I preferred
never to let things go that far. It wasn't that I wanted
to spare myself; it would have been embarrassing for
the others, and I wanted to protect them from that.
And this may explain why later in life I made such a
success of my insurance agency. It was the end-all of
my life, insuring others against the likes of me—the
only goal I had left. But this isn't what I wanted to
tell you, excuse me. I only talk about this because

what I want to talk about is so hard for me to put into words. I've been thinking it through for so many years, as calmly as possible; I never kidded myself. I always refused to rebel against what had happened to me, because from the first I saw that such a reaction made no sense. I wanted to put up with it all without euphemisms, and with as little fuss as possible—that's the only way to do it. Yet how is one to put up with something whose cause escapes one? Or the error one has made? Or which others have made and which one must pay for? I realized that I was condemned to death, of that there was no doubt. Please don't take offense at this expression. I know perfectly well that the law has abolished the death penalty. All the same, I am in the right when I state that I have been condemned to death. And the other prisoners recognize the condemned man. For all they have to do is wait it out, be their sentence for five years or ten or even fifteen; it doesn't matter; but this other is singled out. Something like a chronic case or like a saint, he no longer 'belongs,' but alas he's still there. No one wants to have to look at him; but since that won't do, everyone treats him with exaggerated naturalness. For instance, as in the hospital when one visits someone whom the doctors have given up, one says, 'The minute you're on your feet again, old boy, we'll stow away booze till the very walls reel!' And both smile and both know it's a lie, a matter of good form—neither wants to make it hard for the other.

But ah, when the condemned man smiles, the smile freezes on the faces of the other prisoners. They turn away, they're ashamed, they fancy *they're* guilty somehow. And that's what must be avoided, avoided at all costs! It's a dirty trick. And it's been going on for ages . . . All that was clear to me. And also that there was no Court of Appeal in this case. But I did not know the date on which the sentence would be executed. Often I asked myself, perplexed: What can be keeping them? Sentence has been passed and no one objects to it. This shilly-shallying must be a nuisance for everyone concerned, not just for me. Yet perhaps it lies in the very nature of my crime that they hesitate. That is the only explanation which satisfies my sense of logic, though at bottom it really explains nothing. As for the existence of a crime that requires punishment, I never doubted it a moment; that's why I've never rebelled against my fate. It's simply . . . Now please don't misunderstand me, gentlemen. Naturally, you just thought 'Aha!' because I used the word 'crime,' yet this 'Aha!' of yours won't get you anywhere. I thought I should warn you in advance because otherwise this business will go on much longer, or possibly never come to an end. Now don't take it for arrogance because it's not, it's the result of experience when I state that you could never succeed in uncovering the nature of my crime —or prove it. Because *I* never succeeded and I have had more time for research and certainly had a livelier interest in the results than an examining magistrate or a police detective would have. Oh, if things were only as simple as they believe! I am certain that I have committed a crime; and that here a great deal has come out that would have been better left unsaid, I willingly confess. And all only to be of service to you, gentlemen. I am certain, too, that this crime is very serious; otherwise I would not have been condemned to death, nor would I have had to wait this long for the execution of the sentence, in this awful isolation, which, I suppose, protects the others. All that is clear to me, yet I do not understand the nature of my crime: I don't know when, and I don't know how, and I don't know why. And such a state is—unpleasant . . . And upon very close examination (and I considered such my duty), one sees that the others know about the crime as well; they are taken aback but hold their tongues, since they are equally powerless to prove anything. It must have been a horrible crime! Now you will certainly want to know how *I* know all this. Perhaps you will dismiss it as pure imagination. That would be very nice of you, and I thank you beforehand, but . . . No, that would be like those encouraging words people address to the dying—I brought this up a while back. But to return to your question: Yes, how do I *know?* It's hard to say. One just knows. One knows it awake or asleep; it's a knowledge *of* and *in* the blood. Did I commit it in a state of unconsciousness? That is hardly credible; I have never lost consciousness and actually take as an insult any suggestion that I did. Or could it have been so monstrous a crime (monstrous in my eyes too, and thus past bearing) that the only way out for me was to forget the details? I have read that this happens: one behaves as though it had all been a bad dream; and then it becomes nothing more than a dream which slowly goes fuzzy, leaving only a dull pressure in the region of the stomach. But still . . . Still . . . If that is the case, what else have I forgotten? It's so mysterious, all of it, gentlemen. And who can tell me for sure that I really have forgotten it completely? When I'm least prepared, at the worst possible moment, some detail might come to mind, and there I'd be, defenseless against the pull exerted on me by the past. And this, too. Who can tell me for certain that despite my forgetfulness I have really effectively removed all clues so no one will ever stumble upon them? I might very well have overlooked what seemed at the moment too trivial, only to have it develop with time into the most important of many trivialities. This is what I have been brooding about for so long, but it has always led— nowhere. I have never found a foothold. Nor do I fear unearthing this crime—that might be my salvation. What I do fear is someone coming upon it ahead of me. If, for instance, it were murder . . . You must not take me at my word and start twisting me a rope out of that. Oh, it might as easily be manslaughter, or criminal negligence—and if it is one of those, then there'll be a rainless summer and the pond will go dry and everything will be out in the open. Or the ropes tied to the stones which weighted down my crime will slowly rot and it will rise to the surface. Or bubbles will surprise someone, who will get a pole and investigate. And supposing the element isn't water? What if I buried it? Perhaps the city will run a gas line through that very spot. Or children will be playing cowboys and Indians and choose the self-same spot to dig themselves a hole—and run scream-ing to Mother. Often it's seemed to me things must have reached such a pass. Or very close to it. I'm standing on a corner waiting for traffic to let me walk across. A streetcar rolls past, fast, noisily; it's crowded and the straphangers stand pressed against each other, staring with vacant eyes at the pedes-trians, when suddenly one of them points at me with his free hand (he needs the other for the strap) and shouts: 'There he is!' But of course the streetcar doesn't stop for this, and the other passengers haven't time to turn around and catch a glimpse of me; everything happens so fast, and besides, it's hard to turn around at rush hour. Yes, and what can the man tell the others by way of explanation? I wouldn't know, I'm not in the streetcar. For me, too, all this happens too swiftly; before I've made out what it means, the streetcar disappears around the corner. All that's left is the ringing of its bell . . . I'm stand-

ing there still and everything is as uncertain as before. Those are the times when one breaks out in a
sweat. Out there the world turns on its axis, running
from East to West—and I alone must occupy the
same spot. One gets dizzy from watching, sleep is no
longer sleep. One evening I decided to hunt for my
wife. I traveled the whole night through—I've already
told you this. It was possible that I wouldn't find her,
but I did. I was looking for her because our acquaintance dated from a time that must precede whatever
it is I've forgotten. Strange, isn't it, that I should have
remembered her when the later event has vanished
from memory. And I found her because she was in a
state similar to mine. Not that some crime lay darkly
hidden in my wife's past, as in mine, but that she had
been given up by the medical profession, as I like to
put it. There was no obvious sickness, nothing to convince a hospital, and perhaps it really wasn't a 'sickness'—the word only confuses the issue; the condition may be something else. Believe me, gentlemen,
when I assure you that many more people have been
'given up' than we think. I don't know why, but their
power of attraction on people who haven't yet been
given up is fantastic; nevertheless, from this nothing
evolves but misfortune and annihilation. With us,
though, it was different; we belonged on the same
side. On that side there's nothing left to do but—
watch. For seven long years we were spectators, and
when people came to us for advice we advised them

in the sense that benefited them; for the true spectator judges truer. We never once gave them advice
that would have been proper for ourselves. For example, I insured people!

"Forgive me for keeping you such a long time. It's
clear to me that little of use to a court can come out
of all this. I only felt it necessary to confess these
facts—and *facts* they certainly are—to prevent you
from interpreting the discrepancy between the tone
of my answers and your questions as bad faith on my
part. Before that night with which we are dealing—
in vain, gentlemen, but unfortunately it has so far
been impossible to convince you of this—before that
night, I would have answered you in your own language. After all, I used to be a businessman who
dealt with other businessmen. But my wife's leaving
me . . . Funny, sometimes I believe she's sitting out
there in the courtroom. Or she reads the report of this
affair in the papers and laughs . . . Her leaving me
has changed me completely, and my speech as well.
In a heavy snowfall one does not speak as you would
have one speak. It isn't possible; even trying would
be insane."

The Judge seemed to prefer to ignore this narrative. "Earlier you spoke of a 'chance' which your wife
might have," he said. "Could this mean that you
helped your wife take advantage of this chance? No,
please don't shake your head just yet. By this I mean,
could it be that your wife acted on an agreement to

separate reached previously between you two? In fact, in these circumstances, you might even have seen your wife to the station—nothing really stands in the way of this possibility, as there are trains until almost one. Or there might have been a hired car parked nearby. Perhaps even someone else's car . . . Don't interrupt me, these are only suppositions. In those four hours about which we know nothing, a great deal could have happened, and I only mean to give a little jolt to your memory. I can even give you reassuring news on one point: of course it was necessary for us to investigate the possibility that you and your wife had rowed out on the lake and that there something had happened. But that has been conclusively disproved, since none of the boats were used that night by unauthorized persons. That, by the way, is an extraordinarily strong point in your favor. But let's stay a moment with my suppositions. The decision to separate could have been very sudden, even wordless. It must have been preceded by some painful experience—that there was one, no one can doubt who has followed your testimony. This experience could have been so painful and exhausting that it confused your mind for a time. Thus your memory could have been disturbed—and, too, this snowfall (of which the Court refuses to take cognizance) can be explained, after a fashion."

"That snowfall is a fact," cried out the defendant. "I remember it so clearly."

"Let's drop it for the moment. What I ask you to do is to take a position vis-à-vis my suppositions."

"And the coat?"

"Your wife might have given it away to avoid being easily recognized. It was minutely described in the police report."

"But would she have had the money for another one?"

The Defense emphasized the fact that his client's books had been inspected immediately by a certified accountant. Neither before the event nor thereafter had unusual withdrawals come to light, or anything inexplicable. As for his bank account, as the Court knew, it had been put into the hands of trustees, as it was in the name of the defendant's wife.

The ladies usually have a private savings account —in a piggy bank, say, just for the fun of it. (The Prosecution was in a jocular mood.) Besides, someone could have given her money. Or she had found a job. "By the way, defendant, could you tell us what you plan to do if exonerated by the Court?"

He wouldn't be able to continue his insurance business, replied the defendant. And really, since the house and everything else belonged to his wife . . . Even though she had given him power of attorney; well, he didn't consider it valid any longer . . . "Well, where shall I begin? I, in any case, shall be a burden to no one."

The question hadn't even implied that, said the

Prosecutor, though he would have to admit that this point too—the matter of the property and the defendant's power of attorney in particular—demanded the Court's attention. His meaning had been to learn just what the defendant intended doing *himself* about his wife and her disappearance.

That would be hard to say. For if he were to answer: "Why, nothing at all!" that could only be misconstrued by the Court. And it wouldn't be easy for him either, this undertaking *nothing;* that would be very difficult.

So he wasn't going to hunt for his wife?

No, it wouldn't make sense.

Why wouldn't it?

If the police couldn't find her, how could he? No, it would be insane. She didn't want to be found.

Then he didn't wish to be reunited with his wife?

Oh, *wish!* That wasn't the question.

Well, what was?

Granted that he had them, his wishes were of little importance. All they could do would be injure his wife.

How?

When one shows what one wishes, one only entices the other into an insincerity.

But if he learned that his wife was in difficulties?

Why should she be in difficulties? She had set out in the snow . . .

Wouldn't he leave the snow out of it! The Prosecutor had shouted.

But that's how it had been. It had been her own idea. And presumably she was now—forgive him—beyond the snow . . .

"In short, you won't lift a finger to locate your wife?"

"I will do all I can to keep from doing anything! I will forbid myself action . . ."

"Thank you, at least you answered clearly," said the Prosecutor. "By the way, concerning this particular point, you seem to have changed your mind. The watchman who found you that night beside the lake testified that you were calling her. Can you recall that? Did you call for help?"

No, not for help.

Well, had he called his wife?

Yes, into the snow.

He could drop the snow! Above all, it had been his wish then that his wife hear him?

Yes, why else did a man shout?

Thus he must have supposed his wife was nearby still, within hailing distance?

Yes, certainly. He had looked around for her and she hadn't been there beside him. He had cried out, from shock.

Looked around? Why had he looked around?

That's only a manner of speaking. The snow dis-

turbed one's sense of direction. And, too, he'd probably been thinking about something else for a time.
Yes, that's how it was, but as he looked up . . .

Please go on.

Snow, everywhere snow . . .

Very well, snow. What else?

He had supposed he'd lost his eyesight.

"And that's why you shouted?"

"That, too, perhaps. Yes, just to see if he
could . . ."

"Well, and why else?"

"A person can freeze to death if he sits down and
falls asleep. That's why."

"You feared that something like that might have
happened to your wife?"

"Yes, presumably."

"So you shouted out her name?"

"Yes."

"Often? I mean, you repeated it?"

"I had underrated the snow. This was the first experience I'd had of it . . . Snow kills every sound.
And, then, the direction."

"Which direction?"

"One doesn't *know* which direction . . . I must
have shouted in the wrong direction."

"So you are of the opinion," said the Prosecutor,
"that if your wife had heard you shout, she would
have come back to you?"

"Naturally."

"What seems so natural about that?"

"What else can a person do when he hears his name? Now, of course, it has to be the right name . . ."

"What do you mean by that?"

"I mean I called out the wrong name. It was one she no longer answered to."

"Do you mean to say your wife is living under an assumed name?"

"God, you're back to that . . . That is just one of many superficialities which don't matter. For the police blotter, of course they do, but they don't concern us here."

"I disagree. This is of far greater concern to the Prosecution than, for instance, snow." However, several months had passed since that night. Would the defendant be able now to come up with the name his wife would answer to?

No, replied the defendant—admittedly with much hesitation, and only after glancing through the public. "I would have to see her, then I'd know her name." And then the defendant turned unexpectedly to the Judge: "We are making a mistake, your Honor, if such an expression is allowed me, when we speak of my wife as we have been doing here, as though she were a part of me, an organ. That's no longer so. Possibly it never was entirely, but that's a point we shan't dispute. Now, in any case, it strikes me as completely wrong, and we are making a mistake, too, when we speak of *my* wife. I have searched for her footprints in the snow, but the snow covered them. I called out the name of my wife, perhaps many times (you say four hours, but time's of no importance), and the snow swallowed it up. That's over. This is no way to go about finding another human being. One can find a winter coat, but . . . Yes, even the residue of the tears in that handkerchief was eliminated by the police chemical analysis. It's there the mistake lies."

"Do you often have dreams like the one about the snow?" asked the Prosecutor, obviously to help the Judge out of a difficult situation.

"It was no dream, it was an experience," said the defendant, but without an edge in his voice.

"Very well," said the Judge—he had roused himself sufficiently to take the next step. "I had hoped to spare the Court this snow business, but apparently there's no getting around it. And although I don't expect the explanation to lead us anywhere—just to a further 'snowdrift.' . . . Silence in the courtroom! . . . Defendant, when we asked you earlier why you had reached for your wife's winter coat—upon leaving the house, I mean—you answered that you feared it would be very cold. Were your fears justified? Was it cold?"

"Yes, very cold. My whole body trembled."

"That did not necessarily result from the *exterior* temperature . . . So it was snowing?"

"Yes."

"Did it start immediately? I mean, as soon as you two left the house?"

"I can no longer recall precisely."

"Perhaps the snowflakes whirled against your face and that surprised you?"

"Yes, perhaps . . . But I was never surprised."

"But why not? Not surprised that there was snow at the end of September?"

"No, I don't believe I was surprised."

"Well, what about your wife?"

"Neither was she, presumably. She didn't say anything about it. She walked beside me, but we didn't speak."

"Hmmm! So your wife was walking beside you. Now where were you two going?"

"What do you mean, where?"

"Did you have a destination? Or a chosen direction?"

"We simply followed our noses."

"From the situation of your house, that would have to mean toward the lake. Is that correct?"

"Yes, it might have been like that."

"So you walked through your front yard and then crossed the street into the park that rings the lake?"

"Yes, it might have been like that."

"And when you got to the water's edge, what was it like?"

"I wasn't paying attention. Perhaps the lake was frozen."

"But that really is too incredible! What was it precisely that told you it was snowing?"

"It was there to be seen . . . I can't remember . . ."

"Did the snow stick on your shoulders, for instance, or on your wife's?"

"Of course not. That is, perhaps some did . . . How would I know that now?"

"Your suit was completely dry—next morning, I mean. How do you explain that?"

"How do I explain that? Snow like this really exists . . ."

"No argument about *this* snow," said the Judge in a sort of footnote. "In the face of all these contradictions, you still insist that it snowed?"

"They are not contradictions! You'll understand later . . ."

"Later?" asked the Judge.

"Some day. Perhaps as soon as you get home . . ."

"I have my doubts. And besides, it is the business of the Court to understand *now*. If you would kindly cooperate. Continue your story."

"What story?"

"About the snow."

"Great big snowflakes; very big, and thick. They fell absolutely vertical, very slow, and without a sound. It was very thick. There was no wind at all. That's it, the wind couldn't reach there."

"Where?"

"Where it was snowing."

"Very well. What did you do?"

"What did I do? We walked on, my wife beside me. Not a sound—total calm. Not even our own footsteps. Now that was really a pleasure . . ."

"Why do you say that? I mean, why did you find that so pleasant?"

"Being unable to hear oneself is always a pleasure. And everything was so soft, that might have helped."

"So there must have been snow on the ground?"

"Of course! Wasn't it snowing? And how it snowed! I had to clear a path by scuffing with my shoes, the way children do. The snow was soft and loose—so there was no effort."

"But you weren't wearing the proper shoes for playing in the snow!"

"That's right! I hadn't thought of that . . ."

"You see? And your wife's were even less appropriate. The ladies are in the habit of wearing such thin, open-toed little shoes, sometimes open at the heel as well. If the snow was high, as you just said, your wife must have had very wet feet right away."

"Yes, that's possible."

"I demand that this laughing cease at once!" In his irritation, the Judge had shouted at the public.

"They are rather nervous," the defendant said, nodding in their direction.

"That is no concern of yours. Now then, what about those shoes and wet feet?"

"Yes, it's odd. One doesn't notice things like that."

"You mean, when one has made up one's mind to 'leave'?"

"Yes, something like that."

"So there were no roads?"

"Roads?"

"Yes, roads or paths. Usually people stick to the paths. Even you. And if there were no roads, then perhaps there were houses? Or trees? Or something . . . Perhaps there were lampposts or fences. Or hedges. I don't care what."

The defendant shook his head.

"Oh, and something just struck me: it was night-time, wasn't it; and it was snowing, so the sky was overcast. In fact, it must have been pitch dark. So how on earth could you *see* it was snowing?"

"Yes, that's odd."

"It seems odd to us, too . . ."

"No, perhaps there's nothing odd about it after all. Please, your Honor, just consider this point for a moment. Where does that light come from by which we see our dreams? No one knows, and yet in dreams we see clearly—sometimes even clearer than by day."

"Then you mean that it was all like a dream?"

"Yes, something like . . . Except that one awakens from a dream to find everything as it was."

"Are you absolutely certain that this was no dream?"

As the defendant shook his head again, he smiled. "I would hardly be standing here before you for a dream," he replied.

The Judge seemed to have lost a little of his composure. "You are right about that. All I expect of my questions is that they help you recall this unusual experience. Now then, as you were walking through the snow, did you have the feeling that you might meet another human being? That's how it usually is during a snowstorm; suddenly a silhouette bobs up before us. People almost stumble into each other."

"No, we encountered no one."

"Too bad. It would be so helpful if we had some witnesses. Now, how did this situation strike you? No one just keeps on going further and further into the uncertain. And, add to that, with a woman . . . Either we have a reason for it, or a goal decided upon in advance, or . . . Yes, or it makes us stop and think. A man can lose his way, a man can fail to find an exit . . . You see, I'm trying to imagine this snowstorm . . ."

"No one can, your Honor."

"Well, please help me then. Did you take your wife's arm?"

"No, we just proceeded, next to each other but not touching."

"But then couldn't your wife have stumbled easily?"

"No, everything was so smooth. A broad, flat surface. Like a frozen lake . . ."

"Like a lake? That is interesting. How did you hit on that?"

"Because we had been in the neighborhood of a lake. At least to begin with. And it's only a comparison. Perhaps it wasn't a frozen lake. But it was a surface: broad, endlessly broad. I'm certain."

"Well, wasn't your wife afraid?"

"Not likely. Women, once they've made up their minds, are much less easily frightened than men. But we did not speak."

"Not a word? Well, why not?"

"It was no longer necessary."

"Now listen to me: let's pretend that I am in your situation, with my wife beside me . . . No, it won't work. Doesn't all this strike you as rather cruel?"

The defendant did not answer. His brow was furrowed in some inner effort.

"Do you admit it?" asked the Judge after a short wait.

"Beg your pardon?"

"Admit it was cruel of you?"

"Oh, that! No. Or yes. Perhaps a little bit cruel. But the opposite course . . . It's just like having a headache. One takes a pill if one can't stand it any longer, and soon things seem better. But the headache's still there: somewhere in the background it lies in wait. And one knows this perfectly well at the time, but since pills keep it from hurting, one thinks one's safe."

"Do you often suffer from headaches?" The Judge's question was rather sudden.

"No more often than most people."

"When you do, you take something?"

"Certainly. Why should I torture myself?"

"Do you have a headache now?"

"No, I'm just a little tired."

"And what about that night. Did you have a headache then? Had you taken any pills?"

The defendant smiled. "Really, your Honor, am I never going to be able to make use of a metaphor without being taken literally? Not everything can be translated into legal terminology; and if we insist on attempting it, we will only misunderstand each other. Language wasn't made for such contingencies, and words are usually nothing but pills against a headache. It seems to me that it had simply become unnecessary for my wife and myself to make conversation. We had left the world of words with all its headaches behind us. It was not because of any merits of mine that we had gotten this far; it was I, not my wife, who failed . . . But the snow was the profoundest grace, cool and soft and quiet and lonely. Oh, how totally a man dare entrust himself to such snow! No, there's no reason to fear he will meet anyone, much less collide. There you have it. But I was the one who failed; I wasn't ready for such good fortune. Indeed, I looked behind me, I don't know why. Perhaps . . . Since that night I've had time to think it all through, though thinking things over never helps much . . . Perhaps I, too, would have done well to cry before that. Then all that would have been left of me might have been a handkerchief stained with tears. But I was too much a coward. Too much a coward to renounce all insurance absolutely. That's why I'm standing here giving you so much trouble," he said, smiling. "Yes, all those who look behind them ought to be brought to trial."

"When you speak of this 'looking behind' you," said the Judge, "you mean, don't you, something that happened that night? Would it be more exact to say that you turned around on your way through the snow? And that this is how you lost sight of your wife? Is this correct? She went on, while you turned around? Are we to take it thus?"

"Perhaps I really didn't turn around, though. Who can tell? The snow was everywhere. Not even my own footprints would still be there, they filled so quickly with new-fallen snow. Now that's truly magnificent! Everything white, above and below, to left and right, and without letup the flakes fall. I was asked later how long this had been going on. The watchman asked me and looked at his watch, and the examining magistrate also asked and wrote the figures down. It has been snowing since the beginning of time and will continue forever. Thick white flakes. Between all of us here this snow is also falling. We talk and talk; our words overshoot the mark—and that's why they freeze and finally drop to the ground as peaceful snow. You only need the proper eyes . . . Can't you see it, gentlemen? Between people sitting at one table who wish to communicate across the white cloth, snow falls. One of them asks if the soup tastes good, and the other, across the table, answers: Yes, it's delicious. But steam from the soup plates rises to the ceiling and falls back—as snow. Then the roast arrives. In carving, the knife slips and screeches against the platter while two people discuss the butcher and what he said, the rise in the price of meat. And the news in that day's paper. And how this acquaintance or that lives thus and so, even if it is above their means; whether there'll be another war; well, they will have enjoyed life, some of it, anyway, and have nothing to reproach themselves with. And that nothing is more important than one's health, and so on and so on, for seven years, forever. Words! Words! And it never stops snowing. Snowflakes, thicker and thicker! It makes one dizzy, the eyes close . . . They can no longer see each other, they can no longer hear each other, and that has been so for so long; but they don't get up and run around the table toward each other, they keep right on talking into that snow, each one at his or her end of the table, words, words! The snow would like to give them its gift of loneliness, but they won't accept it. Until they suffocate . . . Did I call the wrong name out of life-long habit? Should I not have called out at all? Did I prove unworthy of that loneliness? Did I betray my one and only chance? Then I ought to be . . ."

Here the transcript breaks off, in the middle of a page and in mid-sentence.